Encouraged By Sparks

By

Gregory Jonathan Scott

DEDICATION

To Scott Burkett, who knows I'd fight any fire for him. I am blessed to have you in my life.

To our Shetland sheepdog, Dylan, who can out-bark a whaling fire alarm any day. He alerts us because he loves us. Unconditionally.

To my father, who understands me completely, and knows why I think he's the greatest man on the planet. I love you, Dad.

To Diane Nelson, for all her ongoing support, cheers and praises.

To Beatriz Zaldivar, whose fascination with *Scorching Hot* firefighters inspired this book.

To the courageous firefighters around the world who risk their lives every day to save the lives of others.

Encouraged By Sparks

Cover Design by Greg J Meier
Cover art is for Illustrative purposes only and any
person(s) depicted on the cover is strictly a model.

Electronic edition also available July, 2015

Published by Gregory Jonathan Scott LLC

http://gregoryjonathanscott.com

https://plus.google.com/u/0/+GregoryJonathanS
cott/posts

https://www.facebook.com/gregoryjonathanscot
tauthor

https://twitter.com/GregoryJonScott

Edited by Tina Adamski, Ally Editorial Services

'Encouraged By Sparks' is a work of fiction. Names,
characters, places and incidents either are the
product of the authors imagination or are used
fictitiously, and any resemblance to actual persons,
living or dead, business establishments, event, or
locals is entirely coincidental.

WARNING: This Book contains material that may be offensive to some, which includes graphic language and adult situations.

Trademark Acknowledgements:

The author acknowledges the trademarked status and trademark owners of the following trademarks mentioned in this work of fiction:

Ghirardelli: Ghirardelli

Macy's: Macy's, Inc. (formerly known as Federated Department Stores, Inc.)

USA Today: USA TODAY, a division of Gannett Satellite Information Network, Inc.

ACKNOWLEDGMENTS

To Tina Marie Adamski. I thank you for your continued
support and blossoming friendship.

A special thanks to the many great friends, authors, readers
and followers that I've established over the past eighteen
months as a writer.
Thanks to, Susan Mac Nicol, Ann Lister,
K-Lee Klein, Sara York,
Kirsty Vizard, Brenda Wright, Jennifer Robbins,
Valerie Degeorge, Toni Hanks,
Tracy Shayler, Alina Popescu, Kimberly Schoeller Kimball,
and so many others.
I am blessed to know you all.

Gregory Jonathan Scott

Chapter 1

Skye left his bedroom and ended his walk in the front room, feeling warmth against the bottoms of his feet that wasn't usually there. He heard commotion outside and there was a distinct odor of scorched timber that made him believe something was burning.

Beyond the front window, he saw rising embers that streaked sparks of light over the brick building across the street and sanctified the wet pavement in front of it. Ochre flames and gray smoke rose in front of him, blocking most of his view from the window he was attempting to see through. All signs pointed to his building being ablaze, burning from the bottom up, flames climbing the walls beneath to get to his apartment.

Skye wore the wide-eyed look of one

entering a pit of doom; fearing for his life. His attention was painstakingly divided between sound and scent, nerves fraying with every step he took.

Smoke swirled upward from the heat vents in the floor, rising higher by the second, quickly casting darkness over the room, mimicking a cobra's sway as if by means of a piper's flute.

Skye ran to the door and reached for the knob, tripping on his sleep pants flapping around his ankles. Before touching the doorknob, he felt the door around it and noticed that it was hot. He pulled away quickly, understanding the hall on the other side must be filled with flames. Back stepping, Skye took off to the window, but fire and thick black smoke rose there now; blocking any hope he had of it being a way out. He sniffed once, twice, and then coughed, propelling poofs of smoke when he did.

The air in the room was getting heavy. Thick smoke poisoned any fresh air remaining, making it harder for Skye to breathe and see.

Skye inhaled floating ash that made his lungs burn. He coughed again, choking a few times, the sound of which blended with an unexpected crash that sounded behind him. He spun in time to see the kitchen floor drop free, opening a trap-door for the fire down below, looking like the gateway to hell.

The smoke filling the room became unbearable, searing Skye's lungs with every breath. Dark soot ringed his nostrils and mouth. Coughing continually, he grabbed a nearby lamp and launched it through the front window, breaking the glass. He blocked the flying pieces by lifting his arms in front of his face before his vision blurred and he went down.

ॐ   ॐ

By the time the rescue team reached the burning complex, the fire had taken over more than half the building, filling the dusky heavens with gray, chalky smoke; virtually concealing the tragedy taking place beneath it.

Orders were given by the captain, directing his team where he needed them, covering all areas in search of survivors and possible casualties. Water hoses stretched out across the ground like fat, slithering pythons, pumping water onto the neighboring structures in an effort to keep them free from spreading fire.

With trained caution, firefighters went into the lower level. When they got inside, the entire level seemed empty, unoccupied, and showed no signs of anybody being there.

Taking the cadet under his wing, lieutenant Emmitt hollered, "Tanner, this way."

Emmitt and Tanner took off around the back of the building, looking for a way to gain entrance to the second level.

Leaving Emmitt at the back of the building using a hatchet to break windows, Tanner headed for the stairs that would take him to the second floor. Cautiously taking one step at a time and testing each one before putting his entire weight on it, the rungs creaked as he climbed, feeling as though they'd break apart beneath his feet despite his vigilance. The hissing of his breath inside the oxygen mask was all he heard, but he kept going and grumbled, "Damn smoke."

The door at the top of the stairway was locked and Tanner felt heat radiating off it from where he was standing. Knowing that waiting could cost lives, he swung the axe, chopping at the door, breaking it down in a matter of seconds. Heat and smoke billowed toward him, rendering him temporarily blind to what was beyond the door.

Creeping forward at a pace that matched a turtle, Tanner walked the hallway until he made it to the front of the apartment, shouting several times, "Fire department. Call out."

No one answered.

Tanner kept going, his helmet-light swept around each room as he looked for anybody still inside. From what he could tell, the fire in this particular apartment seemed to be confined to the kitchen, mostly taking out the floor. The rest of the place seemed to only be filled with smoke, but no visible flames. When he reached the front room, he spotted a man slumped over on the floor, his back against the wall beneath a broken window he may have been trying to exit through.

Pressing his fingers to the man's jugular, Tanner sensed only a light radial pulse and noticed there was limited to no response from the man when spoken to. Tanner called it in, using the radio clipped on his shoulder, "One man down on the second level, front room. Stable but weak."

Tanner picked the man up from the floor, held him tightly against his side and pretty much dragged him down the back steps. Moving in a hurry, Tanner called to the guys coming at him with a water hose, "Coming through. Make a hole."

The man at Tanner's side was weak and he could feel the arm draped over his shoulder sliding down. He hollered again, "Make a hole."

In the street, two medics pushed a wheeled gurney toward Tanner that was meant for the survivor he was half-carrying by this point. An EMT pushed an oxygen mask over the man's grimy face at the same time Tanner eased him carefully onto the gurney.

Tanner leaned in close to the man and asked, "Were you the only one up there? Anyone else with you?"

Skye shook his head weakly.

"Good." Tanner took that as a no and then yelled to the medics, "Get him out of here, away from the smoke."

Abruptly, the man broke into a choking spell and his eyes popped open.

Tanner quickly lifted the mask off Skye's face and helped him sit. "Take slow breaths. It'll be all right."

Skye choked again, gasping harder, and then leaned over the side of the gurney and vomited.

Rubbing Skye's back, Tanner assured him. "That's good, let it out." He waved for the EMT to step in.

As soon as Skye was finished throwing up, he slowly laid back down; the cool sheets against his bare back shocked him. He looked up at the fireman who had pulled him from a burning building and said, "Thanks, I needed saving." He then rolled his head along the mattress, observing his building. "Aw, fuck. My place is toast."

Tanner pushed lazy curls of hair out of Skye's eyes and said, "Lie still and take slow breaths. We'll take good care of you."

Skye blinked a couple of times before lowering his lids to small slits. Keeping his hands locked together in front of him across his chest, he whispered, "Do I need a doctor?"

While the building burned behind him, the EMT searched the man for burns or broken flesh. There were a few spotty injuries, but none that looked to be major.

Tanner fixed the man's twisted pajama pants, putting them in place and said, "You got a name?"

"Skye," he said.

"Good name. I'm Tanner."

"Hello Tanner, and thanks again," Skye said, puffing oxygen.

"You live here?" Tanner asked.

"I do."

"Were you home long?"

"Yeah, for a couple of hours."

"Alone?" Tanner asked again, mostly keeping the questions going to keep Skye alert, making sure his brain activity remained normal.

"Yep. Alone."

Tanner stepped back and let the medic do his job.

The medic adjusted Skye's oxygen hose, tucking it tightly behind his ears and said, "We're going to take you to the hospital. You good with that?"

"Yeah, sure. Do you think I need it?" Skye

winced.

"It's best, just to be sure everything is okay with your lungs. They'll also fix up your burns. You have a few minor ones." The medic wrapped Skye's arm and waist where he noticed the fire had gotten to him.

"Is there anybody we should call?" Tanner asked.

Skye sat up and said, "My phone is in my pocket. I'll handle that." He felt light-headed, which forced him to lie back again.

Tanner laid a hand against Skye's shoulder and told him, "Take it easy, Skye. There's no need to run a marathon just yet. Give your body a chance to get the oxygen back into your bloodstream. That'll take more than a few minutes."

The EMT wrapped Skye's bicep with the BP cuff and asked, "You feeling better?"

"I believe so," Skye mumbled.

Once again, Tanner mentioned to Skye that everything was going to be fine and to do whatever the medic said.

Skye was wheeled to the EMT rescue truck and lifted up inside it.

As he was being locked into place and connected to monitors, Skye saw Tanner standing outside the door looking in. He wondered if Tanner was actually concerned or just liked looking at him.

"Are you planning on taking this trip with me?" Skye lightheartedly asked Tanner.

With a smile, Tanner answered, "I have to stay here for a while, for obvious reasons. But I promise I'll meet up with you later at the hospital."

Skye smiled back, looking into Tanners hazel-green eyes. "You promise?" he asked.

Tanner held two fingers to his temple and saluted. "Yes, I promise."

The doors on the E-unit closed and Tanner walked away.

Chapter 2

The room where Skye was put in the emergency department was cold and bright, the way one would expect. Skye lay in the bed, wired up to various monitors while nurses came and went to observe and take blood, practically sucking him dry. A vampire's true bloody dream.

While Skye lay attached to monitors in the ER, he sent a text message to his dad to let him know what had happened and that he was fine. He'd hardly finished typing the message when his phone rang, and it was his dad, Taggart. Other than having no place to call home when he left the hospital, Skye let his father know there was no real reason to worry. Whatever he owned, which admittedly wasn't much, had burned in the fire, but things could easily be replaced.

His dad's voice rose. "Where is Jimmy? Why isn't he there with you?"

Skye's voice needed to go even higher, putting a stop to his dad's screech. "Tag, I mean,

Dad. Listen. I told you Jimmy and I went our separate ways more than a month ago. It's over. No more."

"How many times have I told you not to call me Tag?" Skye's dad said. "I've always liked him."

"Always? That's funny. It was a four month relationship Pops, doomed from the very first date," Skye snarled into the phone.

"Why's that? He was a good kid and I thought the two of you were a good match… You know what I mean, right?" Tag laughed.

"Match? Nope. We were actually too much alike, making us far from being a good match. Two bottoms don't work in a relationship, just so you know. We both wanted to be the catcher all the time. Always."

"Skyler!" His dad roared, holding a hand over the microphone until his laughter died down to a chuckle.

"What? It's the truth." Skye laughed.

"Okay. Okay. Enough." Tag bounced back quickly. Not that he thought anything was wrong with his son being the receiver in a relationship, but parents don't usually talk to their adult kids about having sex in general and which positions they favor in particular.

When Skye's father sensed his son was okay, he let him go. It was a shorter conversation than usual; but it was a necessary one. They each needed to hear the other's voice to determine if everything was truly fine with both of them. Tag would have been on the road and headed northward to Chicago to be with his kid if he got the sense that Skye was anything but fine. Rain, snow or tornado wouldn't have stopped him from seeing and protecting his child if needed. It's what good parents did.

Two hours after Skye ended his call with his dad; his arm and hip were cleaned up and redressed by one handsome doctor. Like wow-handsome by Skye's standards. The man seemed a bit young to be a white coat, but perhaps he started early due to a bright mind. That piqued Skye's interest for sure. Hooking up with a good looking doctor with a brilliant head on his shoulders was a no-brainer. Skye thought, *Okay, this man will do nicely. I could easily marry him, have babies with him. Could it be I was brought to this hospital for this reason? To meet and marry a handsome doctor, bang his brains out and raise children with him?* Skye sighed when the doctor left the room, wondering if he'd ever see him again. Probably not, but a guy could dream.

Skye's burns hurt, but in the way they would if he had gotten a bad sunburn. Just a little sting was all, really. Nothing more. Nothing less. He could handle a bit of a fiery pang in his side. What he was having trouble dealing with was where he was going to go when released from the hospital. A hotel would work for a few nights, but then where to?

Skye was getting antsy lying in bed doing nothing. What he really wanted was a bath to wash away the charcoal colored pigment coating his pale skin. He looked at the clock again, noticing that four hours had gone by since he arrived. Why were they keeping him so long? What was going on?

Thirty more minutes had passed and during that time Skye stared out the floor to ceiling glass wall in front of him. He was looking for the firefighter who saved his life to be wandering the halls of the ER. Where was he? He promised he'd meet him at the hospital.

Skye suddenly felt relief when the same doctor who fixed him up earlier came back into the room. He reviewed the records of Skye's monitors one last time, and then told him the nurse would be in shortly to discharge him.

Skye was happy about that, but also expressed some concern about leaving because he had no place to go.

Waiting in the bed, rapping his fingers against his bare chest, Skye wondered how he was going to get where he needed to go wearing nothing but choo-choo train pajama bottoms and an open-back hospital gown. Walking down the street like that would certainly turn a few heads and most people he passed would think he was freaking nuts.

First stop: Macy's department store for some respectable clothing and fashionable footwear. That was a given.

Interrupting Skye's plans for his life after the ER, a nurse walked into the room carrying a handful of papers including a list of organizations for him to reach out to if he was in need of any help. He also gave Skye the firehouse details in order to contact them if he needed to. His nervous heart settled a bit when he received the phone number for the firehouse and secretly hoped Tanner would be the one who answered his call when and if he made it.

The lights just got a little brighter.

Just then, Tanner shuffled through the

doorway, all cleaned up and looking hotter than hell in his firehouse blues, an overnight bag in one hand and a box of chocolates in the other. When Tanner saw Skye looking better than he had a few hours ago, even though still covered in soot, he wasn't able to control the bright, toothy smile that appeared.

Skye's eyes lit up like auburn fireballs and a huge grin enhanced his face. "Hey, you came. Thank God. I was getting lonely."

"I told you I would." Tanner smiled wider and it enriched his face the same way Skye's auburn eyes sparkling enhanced his own.

"You made it just in time. I'm being released, like right now." Skye moved to the chair beside the bed so he could distance himself from being the injured victim. He hated that feeling and wanted to be in control of himself straightaway.

Tanner pushed the box of Ghirardelli chocolates he brought as a get well gift toward Skye. "For you," was all he said.

"Oooo, Dark Twilight Delight chocolates are my favorite. I love these." — Skye paused and looked crookedly at Tanner — "Wait… Is this some kind of pun because my skin is a bit darker than usual right now?"

"That's fitting. But no." Tanner smirked.

"Doesn't matter, these are the best. You want one?" Skye held the box in front of him.

"Maybe later."

"Okay. Suit yourself."

"These are for you, too." Tanner tossed the overnight bag on the bed.

"Please tell me there are clothes in that bag."

Skye reached for the bag and unzipped it.

"Hope they fit, but in a pinch; I'm sure they'll do fine."

"Who cares? I just need street clothes." Skye pleaded, "Would you be so kind and close the drapes. Don't want anybody seeing my junk and stuff."

"Yeah, sure." Tanner closed the drapes and then walked to the door. "I'll be right outside." He grabbed the handle and started backing out.

"What are you doing? Don't be silly. You can stay," Skye protested, while reaching into the satchel for the change of clothes.

Acting casual, Tanner stepped back into the room and closed the door. His heart raced. Not because he was working up a sweat closing drapes and shutting doors, but because he was nervous about seeing Skye, whom he was attracted to, get undressed in front of him. The idea alone heightened his anxiety and sent his heartbeat into overdrive.

Holding up what looked like the same T-shirt Tanner had on, Skye said, "Is this one of yours?"

"Yep, it is. I was in a hurry to get over here, so I just grabbed what was within reach," Tanner said. "It might be a bit large, but it'll do for now."

Skye put it on, taking in Tanner's scent as he did. His lids fluttered. He liked it.

Watching Skye's reaction, Tanner smiled. That's it, just smiled.

Then Skye dropped his bottoms and kicked them aside. Everything below his waist exposed.

Tanner looked away, glancing at the walls, the ceiling, and then the heart monitor that had flat-lined, not reading anything. His heart beat even faster than before; he felt it in his throat.

"I'm not sure I really want to know, but how does my apartment look?" Skye asked.

"A blackened pile of rubble that's not a place you can go back to," Tanner warned. "The marshal has it roped off for investigation."

"Investigation!" Skye shrieked, pulling up the jeans Tanner brought.

"Don't worry. That's normal practice. Every fire gets investigated to figure out how it started." Tanner watched Skye adjust himself inside his jeans, impressed by what he saw; he forced himself to look away.

Skye gathered up the papers the nurse carried in and handed them to Tanner. "Here, look through these and let me know if you find a hotel or B&B that would be suitable *and* cheap. I need a place to stay for a few days until I can get things straightened out with the insurance broker."

Tanner fanned them out across his hand, rapped them against his palm before making a suggestion to Skye. "Hey listen... You can stay with me for as long as you need. I have room."

"I couldn't do that to you. You have a life and I wouldn't feel right about intruding on your family," Skye said, pulling on a pair of socks.

"You don't have to worry about that. I live alone. No family to intrude upon," Tanner assured him.

Skye tied his borrowed shoes and added, "What about a canine buddy? Do you have one who would chew my bones during the night?"

Tanner laughed. "No dog. Or cat. You'll be

fine."

"I suppose staying with you would simplify my situation while giving me time to reorganize my shit." Skye stood and tucked his choo-choo pants into the satchel.

Tanner teased, "Okaaay, those are adorable. Are they a childhood treasure?"

"Cool it. No making fun of my favorite PJs." Skye ran a hand down his chest, ending with a cupped hand over his crotch. "Can't you see all this would never fit into any childhood jammies?"

"I took note." Tanner grinned.

Right after Skye smirked at Tanner for noticing how nicely he'd grown up, he felt light-headed again and dropped back into the chair before he hit the floor.

Concerned, Tanner helped him sit. "Hey, you okay?"

"I just felt dizzy. I think I'm fine," Skye responded.

"Stay put. I'll call in the nurse," Tanner ordered.

The doctor came in through the door ahead of the nurse and told Skye he needed to stick around a while longer. They didn't want him going anywhere just yet.

When Skye was first brought in, his blood showed nutritional deficiencies and the X-ray of his lungs were cloudy. The doctor ordered the tests again to see how Skye had progressed over the past few hours, make sure he was clearing up.

The nurse hung the therapy bag on the IV pole above Skye's head and then told him, "It won't be long, just a few more tests to run."

While waiting for results and hopefully release papers, the ER quieted down quite a bit. Tanner went ahead and dimmed the lights in Skye's cold room in an effort to make the atmosphere as relaxed as he could. It seemed to work, they fell asleep side by side, Skye in bed while Tanner stretched out in the chair next to him.

The doctor crept in a short time later, waking Tanner first with a shake to his shoulder. Blinking a few times, Tanner was surprised to find his hand gently locked with Skye's. When that had happened, he wasn't quite sure. During his dream state. Possibly.

The nurse who followed the doctor in smiled when he saw the compassionate connection, thinking the two made a cute couple and wondered if they were married.

Skye blinked a few times before his eyes sprang open; when his vision cleared he sat up quickly and spotted the nurse and the doctor standing over him. Behind them, Tanner stood cross-armed by the door, staring.

"Is everything okay?" Skye worried, squinting one eye, still trying to adjust that one to the light that was shining down behind the doctors head.

"You're fine now," the doctor said. "You're good to go, but take it easy over the next few days."

When they left the hospital, the feverish wind that was present earlier had settled, almost as if it were telling them everything was going to be all right.

Chapter 3

While riding shotgun next to Tanner in his pickup truck like they were a couple of macho men on a hunting trip, Skye's expression suddenly went blank when he thought about his entire life flashing before his eyes. It came upon him as a delayed reaction. That type of thing normally showed up during the event and he wasn't expecting it to hit him like that. The speed show put him in an instant state of shock.

Tanner glanced at Skye, picking up on his abrupt mood change. He hadn't known Skye long, but the perplexed expression strangling the color from his complexion was a sign to Tanner that the trauma of the day's events had just set in.

There was a slight pause and Skye's moonlit face bloomed and then contorted. His mouth opened until it would have taken in a king-sized apple. "Oh... Oh my Gawd, I was almost killed today. Burnt to a crisp. If you hadn't come along when you did, I just might be learning how to use a set of wings right about now." His hands nervously stroked his thighs, palms heating up as they slid back and forth from hip to knee. He gasped and then slumped back in the seat, rolling his head across the headrest to face Tanner. "I think I'm going to hurl again."

Tanner's hand rested on Skye's, slowing down his anxiety. "Everything is fine. You're okay to go home by the doctor's orders."

Skye breathed and his voice lowered. "What am I going to do now? Where am I going to go? I have nothing."

Tanner moved his hand to the nape of Skye's neck and massaged it. His voice turned gentle. "Listen. Don't sweat it right now. You're not alone and you can hang at my place for as much time as you need. I have plenty of room for two and I'll help you out no matter how long it takes."

"Thanks, Tanner. That's good Samaritan-like of you."

"That's just how I am. Why do you think I became a firefighter? I have this uncontrolled need to help people no matter what is or isn't in it for me." Tanner stroked Skye's neck with one last squeeze and then placed his hand back on the steering wheel. "Are you good—for now?"

Skye's glowing auburn eyes stared back at Tanner, lashes fluttering a couple times before he said, "I'm good. Thanks for being here. It means a lot."

"All right then, homeward bound." Tanner stepped on the gas pedal, pushing the pickup truck a little faster.

"How far do you live from here?" Skye

asked.

"Just a few blocks up ahead," Tanner answered, pointing to the right. His home stood in Downers Grove, an older neighborhood a few miles west of downtown Chicago. It was quite close to the hospital Skye had been at and not too far from where his apartment went up in flames. They were practically neighbors.

Chicago is a large city, so there was no surprise that Skye and Tanner hadn't run into one another before. Neither of them were bar hoppers, mostly because they were too involved in their careers to be picking up strangers at the downtown nightclubs.

Unfortunately, it took a spark to bring them together. By way of smoke and flames, Tanner the firefighter met Skye the architect.

They pulled into Tanner's driveway, headlights sweeping the lawn before the beams settled on the garage door. Skye admired the small Tudor-style home with cedar shingled siding and deep pine entry door. It suited Tanner, seemed fitting for a fireman. The stacked stone chimney towering past the sharply sloped roofline was a quaint touch. It added warmth to the home, in addition to giving it a sweet, storybook charm. Skye thought it was masculine-cute, if that made sense, and couldn't wait see inside.

Rattling the keys in the front door, Tanner opened it, inviting his guest to precede him, saying, "After you."

Glancing around the front room, Skye saw what he'd expected he would. It was decorated in warm tones like the outside; inviting, neatly organized, not too cluttered, and it was clean.

Tanner started out by saying, "This is the living room, and up ahead is the dining, kitchen and sunroom." He took the overnight bag from Skye and led him further into the house.

To their right was a short hallway that led to the master bedroom and bath. Tanner didn't take Skye down that hall, just pointed it out to him mentioning where it headed. Upstairs were two more bedrooms with a single Jack-and-Jill bathroom connecting them. Doors on either side of the bath opened into each bedroom. The sloped ceiling that mimicked the roofline outside made both bedrooms feel cozy.

"We can put you in one of these rooms," Tanner said, dropping the satchel on the bed.

"This one actually should work okay, since you just added the bag to it." Skye smiled.

"I'll get you a towel, because you look and smell like you need a shower." Tanner winked at Skye before heading to the hallway linen closet, then spoke loudly. "Everything else you need is in the bathroom on a shelf, in a cabinet or in the shower. If you can't find what you need, let me know."

"A toothbrush and toothpaste would do nicely," Skye hollered back.

Returning to the doorway of the bathroom, Tanner held out a fresh towel and tried his damndest not to stare at Skye's chest when he removed his shirt. Tanner's thoughts bottomed out and he finally said, "Um—there should be a few new toothbrushes in the drawer to the left of the sink. I keep a stash of them in there, toothpaste too."

"Great," Skye said, pulling the drawer open.

Tanner stepped into the bathroom next to Skye, standing so close he could feel the heat rising from his bare chest. His voice went low. "Why don't you let me help you remove these bandages? It'll be easier for me to do it than you fumbling with them yourself. When you're finished showering, I can fix you back up again."

"That's okay," Skye said, picking at the tape stuck to his arm. "I can get them off easily enough, but I will take you up on your offer at putting me back together."

Tanner winked and backed away. "Sure."

"You know, I really appreciate what you're doing for me, Tanner. There aren't many people like you who would open up their home for a stranger."

"Meh, I don't mind," Tanner said. "Glad I can help you out. For some reason you don't feel like a stranger."

"Okay, then." Sky spun around. "Is there anything I need to know in order to operate your shower?" Skye asked, pulling back the linen curtain.

"Nope. Just pull and turn. Everything else will happen naturally." Tanner leaned a shoulder against the doorjamb, and smiled at Skye, taking in his beautiful eyes the way he did when he first saw them. They drew him in like he was under a hypnotic spell, struggling with tearing his gaze away. They were that beautiful to him, as stunning as the rest of Skye.

Skye looked back, letting the sparkle in his

eyes captivate Tanner. He knew they were. He could tell by the way Tanner was looking through him, like all he was seeing were his eyes.

Shaking his gaze from a dreamy trance, Tanner said, "One more thing. You look great with your beard shadow coming in, but if you need a razor, there should be some of those in the drawer below the toothbrushes."

Skye glanced into the mirror, looking at his dirty face and replied, "Since you like it like this, I'll leave the scruff alone."

"Excellent. I'll put some clean clothes for you to wear on the bed. See you in a few. I'll be down stairs." Turning away, Tanner pulled the door closed until it latched.

Chapter 4

Cheerfully whistling in the kitchen while hearing the shower running in the bedroom above his head, Tanner pulled out one of his better bottles of wine and two crystal glasses that chimed when he placed them on the stone countertop. The warm-bodied Shiraz he chose was one of his favorites, and he hoped Skye would enjoy it too. He popped the cork to let it breathe.

As promised, Tanner gathered fresh gauze and triple antibiotic ointment for Skye's burns. He placed them on the table in the dining area before diming the lights and heading back to the kitchen; where he stood waiting for Skye to come down. Hopefully shirtless, the way he liked him.

Still upstairs in the bathroom, Skye stood in front of the mirror with an oversized smile on his face that slowly went crooked and then flattened.

He stared at himself, doubting that a gorgeous firefighter like Tanner could be interested in someone like him. Even though Skye had been told he was a good-looking man more than a few times, he still saw plenty of room for improvement. He checked out his own reflection, looked it up and down while flipping his fingers through his wet cocoa-colored hair. A few loose strands fell back across his forehead, giving him a reckless but sexy appearance, like a rebel without a cause.

He inhaled, removed the towel from around his waist and walked naked to the bedroom to get dressed. What he found laid out on the bed was nice, but he really wanted the choo-choo pants he adored so much and felt comfortable in. He pulled on a pair of dark blue sweatpants, tugged the legs halfway up his shins, kept his feet bare, and put on a clean blue T-shirt with the red fireman's seal on each shoulder. It must have been one Tanner didn't wear anymore; it was well worn and had shrunk too small for a man of Tanner's size. It fit Skye a bit snugly and showed off his well-chiseled chest rather nicely. He circled the collar a few times with his fingers, stretching it so he could breathe a little easier. He felt good in the fireman's blues, like he'd climbed a few notches on the macho scale. He felt butch, well more butch than usual, anyway.

When he realized what he was doing, he started to tremble. His confidence dwindled when he thought again that Tanner seemed too perfect for someone like him. His attraction to Tanner had grown quickly throughout the day and he couldn't understand why Tanner, if he did, found him attractive. There must be hundreds of gorgeous men undoubtedly knocking on Tanner's door. When he compared himself to what he imagined Tanner wanted, he found himself to be in short supply of whatever that was.

He finally broke eye contact with his reflection and stepped away from the looking glass in order to prevent the self-doubting scenario from going any further. It would only bring down an evening that was headed upward. He lingered a few more moments before leaving the bedroom, tugging again at the constricting collar.

Skye flipped the light switch off. The room slowly dimed, converting it back to a dark empty space. He closed the door and proceeded down the short hallway, pausing a moment when he reached the top of the stairway to peer out the window. His gaze penetrated his own transparent image reflecting back at him while he fancied the glowing lap pool down below in Tanner's back yard. Shaking the image away, he spun around and headed downstairs to join Tanner, his very-well-could-be boyfriend. With that thought, Skye's smile found its way back to his face.

ക   ൞

As luck wouldn't have it, Skye came down with a shirt on. Disappointed yes, but Tanner could always have the pleasure of ripping it off him.

"You look better. How do you feel?" Tanner said, gawking while trying not to look obvious about it.

"Not bad," Skye replied, wincing slightly as he held the shirt off his skin where the fire had gotten him. "I had to run the shower cool to ease the sting of my burns. That hot water was like a shark attack and the bitch wouldn't let go."

Trying not to laugh at Skye's description of his traumatic experience in the upstairs shower, Tanner bit his cheek. "Come with me. I've got pain relieving ointment and some fresh wrap. I'll take care of you."

Skye followed Tanner into the dining room and then back to the kitchen where the light was brighter. "Uh, I could have just stayed here you know."

"You're amusing, now get over here and stand in the light so I can see what I'm doing. Lift the shirt or take it off," Tanner ordered, crossing his fingers that the shirt would disappear.

"Which would be easier? On or off?"

"Off, but you decide."

"Aren't you the doctor? It should be your call."

"A doctor no, but I'm supposed to be a professional here. If I had it my way, I'd want it off." Tanner screwed the heel of his hand into his temple, shook his head and added, "To make it easier… is why. Yes… so it's easier for the both of us."

"Then it comes off. Totally professional, I got it."

Tanner swallowed hard when Skye lifted the shirt up over his head, exposing his rolling abs and smooth pumped up chest. He gulped harder when he saw the leafy tattoo traveling over his left shoulder and down across his pectoral. There was something about a man with a tattoo that made his dick go stiff.

"Okay, all yours. Do your doctoring," Skye puffed, when he lowered his arms, but then lifted them again so Tanner could work magic around his waist.

"Hold still and try not to flinch." Tanner put on a rubber glove and squeezed some ointment on a few fingers.

Skye grinned and said, "Hey. Shouldn't we get to know each other better before you go probing my body with a couple of slippery fingers?"

"What? Professionalism, remember? Don't make me laugh." Tanner's voice went gritty. "Stand still so I don't hurt you."

"Yes, sir."

"And don't call me sir. I'm sure we're close to the same age and sir makes it sound like I'm much older."

"Okay, sir."

Rolling his eyes while getting down on his knees, Tanner gripped Skye's hip to hold him steady. With his gloved hand, he gently dispersed the ointment over the burn at the side of Skye's ribcage. He noticed how hard his body was beneath his grasp and he liked it. Keeping himself professional like he said he would, Tanner tried to concentrate on the wound he was tending instead of the hairy trail that climbed Skye's six-pack abs and called it quits halfway between his navel and chest.

"That feels better already." Skye wiggled when he talked.

"Hold still so I can finish. I'm almost done."

Tanner wrapped the gauze around Skye's waist, bringing it just below his ribcage, hiding that hairy six-pack he liked so much. When he reached around Skye's back for the end of the gauze to bring it back around to the front, all he could think about was pulling Skye against him and kissing him. He told himself again, *keep it professional.*

"You have nice hair," Skye pointed out, a little giddy about seeing only the top of Tanner's head. That was a view he could get used to, Tanner taking care of business while assuming the position on his knees in front of him.

As Tanner stood up, looking directly into Skye's eyes the entire time, he said, "Hold your hand right here while I tape everything into place." He pointed to the end of the gauze at Skye's side.

"Looks good," Skye said, replacing Tanner's hand with his own.

"Lift your arm." Tanner copied what he did to Skye's waist, only this time while standing. "Okay, done. You can put your shirt on."

"Are you sure?" Sky asked, a little coyly.

"Yes, I'm sure. I need you to put your shirt on," Tanner pleaded, sweat beads forming at his furrowed brow.

Skye grinned.

"Would you like a little wine?" Tanner asked.

"Only if it comes with refills."

Chapter 5

Tanner woke the next morning with his usual daybreak hard-on, stone-stiff and aching for a whole new reason. He was harder than granite because he had Skye on his mind, which led him to wanting Skye on his dick, riding it like a bronco stud until he got his rocks off up inside the guy's ass. Tanner thought about Sky while joyously whacking his willy until he shot cum all over his bare chest and face. He let out a good-sized load, similar to the way a hose douses fires. It was his usual spectacular discharge that needed a beach towel to clean up.

At the same time Tanner was blowing his hot wad downstairs, Skye was upstairs doing who knows what. Probably still sleeping or holding back the noise of his own lustful session of self-pleasure.

Even though Tanner brought out in Skye the massive urge to pump and dump a load, Skye refrained from bopping the bologna out of respect for being in somebody else's home. That just wouldn't be right. Not yet anyway.

Before the sun had a chance to take over the sky completely, Tanner had left for the firehouse to pull off his usual duties of being a hero. The normal stuff firemen do; saving lives, dousing fires, bickering with his house brothers and then loving them a minute later.

With the rising sun, Skye was making an effort at waking too. After rolling out of bed, he quietly busied himself, trying to be respectful of Tanner, thinking he was downstairs, and possibly still sleeping. Because the first floor seemed quieter than expected, Skye went down to see if Tanner was awake and he himself being politely quiet.

There was no Tanner anywhere, his truck was gone, and on the kitchen counter Skye found a note that said, *'I had such a good time with you last night, Skye, that it slipped my mind to tell you I had to work today. Sorry about that. You're welcome to anything in the house, food, drink, rest and most of all, relaxation. Take it easy and enjoy your day, but try to stay out of my bedroom, I have secrets in there that only I should know about. (Sinister laugh goes here). Okay, that was corny. Ignore that please. Anyway, I'll be gone until tomorrow afternoon. That's how things work when you're a damn hot freakin' fireman. Oh, Gawd, another bad attempt at being humorous. Ignore that too please. I'm not hot, just a simple fireman. You'll have to get used to that, my stupid humor that is, and the schedule of a firefighter. We work a couple of days and then we're off a few. It's great, actually and I hope you can adapt. FYI: All emergency phone numbers are on the refrigerator door including my personal cell number. If you need to, please call me. Actually, I'd like it if you would. Oh by the way, you never gave me yours so I look forward to seeing you when I get home so you can give it to me then. I hope this doesn't buzz your skull, but here goes - LOLove and I can't wait to see you again. Tanner.'*

Skye didn't just smile at the letter Tanner left; he grinned, and held it to his chest, drawing in the scent Tanner had left all over it. It was intoxicating and the thought of him wrenched his stomach with a flash of nerves that made it clear he really liked him. All of him. From bottom to top.

The letter was a cute attempt at breaking the ice of a new, albeit unintentional relationship, and Skye loved it. Putting the love note in his pocket, Skye turned to the refrigerator and added Tanner's phone number into his own cell, saving it as a favorite right after adding a quick-link to his phone's desktop.

Skye had a dreamy look on his face, probably looked ridiculous but he didn't care, he was gleefully crushing, sort of happy at the moment and in a sick sort of way, he was glad his apartment turned to toast. Because it did, giving him his new love interest, who was hotter than the fire he rescued Skye from.

An idea came to Skye while he basked in the glory of the sweet letter from the man he just met. Remembering the location of Tanner's firehouse was listed in the pile of papers the nurse at the hospital gave him, Skye scrammed upstairs to go through it. He rifled through the stack like a madman, eventually finding the address he was looking for.

There was a long pause before Skye made his next move; his bright idea was to show up unannounced at the firehouse with a gift of thanks. Was it a good idea or a stupid one? He shook his head and said, "What the hell."

While waiting for a cab to arrive, Skye searched the route to the firehouse on his smart phone, looking for a bakery to stop at on the way. His eyes lit up when he found a cupcake shop about halfway there and then he said, "Perfect, who doesn't like cupcakes."

Chapter 6

On his way, sitting in the backseat of the cab, Skye helped himself to a few select cupcakes he'd picked up for himself while sipping on the hot coffee he'd also gotten.

As the cab approached the fire station, Skye edged closer to the window and looked out, hoping Tanner was there and not on a heroic rescue so early in the day. The first thing he saw was the fire trucks parked inside the stations garage. In front of each door were several pairs of boots standing at the ready. That being seen, Skye took it as a good sign Tanner was in the house.

Walking around to the back of the fire truck was a tall muscular man. As Skye watched him, figuring he was another fighter of fire, he said, "Holy shit, he's hot too."

Skye pushed the door of the cab open with his foot while balancing the box of mini cupcakes in one hand and his cup of hot coffee in the other. "This is it," he said. "The place Tanner turns into a hero."

The firefighter hanging alone in the garage set down the oxygen cylinders he was carrying. Walking to the front of the truck, he wondered what the unknown man was doing there with what appeared to be a box of doughnuts. At first, he only watched Skye awkwardly shimmy from the cab before he decided to go help him.

Around the corner with a smile on his face came Flash, the station's pet. He wasn't the typical spotted Dalmatian that would have been stereotypical, but a perky sheltie. The small dog met every visitor that came to the house, approving and then welcoming them. Anybody he decided wasn't welcome would be corralled to a corner like a barnyard sheep.

As soon as Skye turned from the cab, he met the fireman face to face, almost bumping into him while tripping on the dog.

Standing, staring at Skye, the firefighter said, "Good morning, can I help you?"

Skye looked him in the eyes. "Um... Well. I came to see and thank Tanner."

"Sure. And you are?"

"Skye. My name is Skye."

"I see. I'm Dalton."

Skye thought, *Of course. Another hot guy with a great name. Can it get any better?*

"Follow me. I'll take you to Tanner. You want help with those?" Dalton asked.

"If you wouldn't mind." Skye passed the box to Dalton while the dog of the house trotted cheerfully at their side.

Inside, Tanner was sitting in the kitchen on a

stool that faced the door. When he saw Skye and Dalton walk through it, a puzzled look crossed his face and he stood.

Skye saluted and smiled.

"Hello. What brings you here?" Tanner asked, walking up to Skye, bending to pat Flash on the head as he passed him.

Everyone else who was seated around the room turned to see what was going on, some of them stood.

Skye glanced at those he was able to see over Tanner's broad shoulders and quietly said, "I came to thank you guys for helping me out of that fire yesterday. I hope everyone likes mini cupcakes."

Dalton carried the box to the countertop and opened it up. "That was awfully kind of you, but you didn't have to do that."

Flash followed, lifting his nose in the air, getting a whiff of what was in the box and hoping it was all for him.

Tanner stayed with Skye, while the guys charged for the box like hungry bulls, and someone with an Irish brogue said, "Weeze love cupcakes, don't ya know."

Without moving, Skye said to Tanner, "Was it okay that I came to see you?"

"Of course it was," Tanner said. "We get visitors in here all the time, so this is no big deal. Come on in and meet the guys."

Tanner and Skye moved into the kitchen where the fired-up brotherhood were making pigs of themselves over the box of mini cupcakes while Flash was catching every crumb before it hit the floor.

Tanner introduced Skye to everyone as well as them to him. It turned into a meet and greet that seemed like Tanner was getting approval from both sides.

Skye thanked them all for lugging him from the fire and accepted their "don't mention its" as if saving a life was no big deal. It was huge to him, even though they acted like they were there to just move furniture. As Skye watched them, he could tell they were a close group, he'd heard about the kind of connection many firefighters had before he got there. It was a family in the house. A brotherhood.

Figuring Skye was a new hookup of Tanner's, the guys greeted him with grins while they waggled their brows at Tanner. Considering that, they would surely harass and rib Tanner as soon as Skye left the building. The guys were like that and it was part of the deal for introducing a fresh sweetheart into their circle of men.

With a mouth full of cake and frosting, someone said, "Damn these are good. Thanks for bringing them in, Skye."

Smiling at Skye and then winking at Tanner, Emmitt said, "Damn delicious is what these are. Thank you, Skye. Come back anytime, ya hear."

While the station brothers consumed every mini cupcake without taking a second to breathe, Tanner gave Skye a tour of the firehouse the same way he did with grade school wannabe firefighters. Tanner led Skye from the kitchen, walked him through the great room where the guys mostly hung out, pointed out the sleeping quarters and then finished the tour in the garage where they ended up between the two trucks. Alone.

Skye seemed intrigued, even a bit fascinated by everything he saw. The constant smile and wandering eyes showed evidence that he was. The smile could have been because he was with Tanner again.

Tanner asked Skye how he got there without a car.

Answering Tanner like a smart-ass, Skye gave up the secret that cabs in the city were at everyone's disposal. Anytime. Day and night. He sniggered and leaned back against the red truck nonchalantly with a surreptitious glance. His eyelids flickered, pulling Tanner in.

The space between them was squeezed away when Tanner advanced a step forward and pressed a palmed hand against the truck above Skye's head, leaning into him, breathing the same air. Tanner shyly looked down at his feet and then back up into Skye's eyes and said, "I'm glad you came. For me it was a great surprise. And as you could tell, the guys loved the baked goods you brought with you. We don't get many people thanking us for what we do, so it was nice that you did."

"No big deal, it was the least I could do after what you and the guys did for me yesterday. I also wanted to see you again and I didn't think I could wait until tomorrow night." Skye looked back at Tanner, into his eyes and then at his lips. They were slim and sweet looking, and to feel them pressed against his own would be the best way for Tanner to repay his good deed of treating the house.

A brush with endearment came between

them while alone in the garage. A hug would have been nice, a kiss even better. Just in time and before doing something they might regret later; footsteps echoed in the garage, breaking them apart.

It was Emmitt. "Whoa, guys." He held up his hands when he saw Tanner and Skye between the two trucks. "Sorry. Carry on." He backed away.

Tanner turned. "Wait. It's not what you're thinking." *Not yet anyway.*

Emmitt smirked and hummed to himself, "Mmm-hmm."

Skye took a minute to digest Tanner's reaction, deliberating if it was exactly what Emmitt was thinking and if that was what Tanner wanted to happen.

Tanner turned back toward Skye and grinned. "Aw, shit. I've got some 'splainin to do."

"What do you mean?" Skye asked.

"This. You and me." Tanner's finger bounced from his chest to Skye's.

Skye cocked his head, mulling over the idea of lunging at Tanner's mouth with his own, but he held back.

Tanner admitted, "Honestly speaking, Skye. It was what Emmitt thought. I wanted to steal a kiss from you just then. There, I said it."

Surging stomach or not, Skye was crazy happy when he heard Tanner's confession. He said, "Be that thief. You still can and I wouldn't mind a single bit if you did."

Tanner took a silent breath, tilted his head to make his move.

Skye closed his eyes and waited.

Just then, the fire bell rang, ending Tanner

and Skye's first kiss before it began.

Both startled by the sudden clang, their eyes sprang open and they backed away.

"Shit! I've gotta go." Tanner's hand stroked Skye's jaw as he skipped backward out of site.

"Son-of-a-bitch!" Skye grumbled. "So fucking close."

Seconds after the horn blew, firefighters rushed the garage as though the gate at the running of the bulls in Pamplona had opened, every beast behind it hitting the alley.

Like one of the participants, Skye quickly ran to get away from the charging bulls.

Everything happened so fast! Within seconds, the fire trucks busted the gates and took to the streets with sirens blaring.

Tanner saluted Skye as the truck passed by him, then came the wink.

Hesitantly, Skye waved goodbye. It was so disconcerting to watch Tanner race away to fight a fire or whatever it was he was called away to do. Deep down, Skye already hated it.

Chapter 7

Skye watched the skyline out the side window of the cab as it made the trip back to Tanner's house; the only place he had to stay at the moment. A light wind blew through the thin gap at the top of the window, tugging at strands of his hair and snapping them across his forehead.

During the ride, Skye had a sudden uneasy feeling that made his heart pause and his stomach churn. It was a feeling he'd heard about and dreaded, the feeling that came when a dearly loved one was taken down in the line of duty. He fought the thought of Tanner being injured on the job, or worse—killed. Regrettably, that possibility was in the cards for a firefighter. If it upset Skye this much now, how could he live with worrying day after day? Getting involved with a firefighter would take a toll on him.

Interrupting his rambling thoughts, he remembered his car was still sitting along the side street next to his burnt apartment. It was the only thing he owned and he'd definitely need it. Instead of going back to Tanner's house, Skye asked the driver to make a U-turn and take him to where he'd left it.

There was nothing like having a set of wheels in Chicagoland. Not only could Skye come and go as he pleased without having to wave down a driver or wait for the train, it also gave him his independence.

After a few errands in his own car, he finally made it back to Tanner's house and went inside to hopefully set his mind at ease. He really needed that after the couple of days he had. Rest, relaxation, and maybe a mind-altering drink or two would help.

In the meantime, the fire truck Tanner was in headed to a house that was going up in flames. It was down a street considered to be nothing more than a waste-land, in a rundown neighborhood where the residents were more concerned about finding their next fix than being an upstanding citizen with a paying job. The place was familiar to the firefighters; they'd been down that road before. Like many times in the past, the people set their own homes on fire while setting sparks to a pipe filled with Marijuana or crack. Lighting up a stogie to smoke while lounging on the floor next to an old set of drapes was never a good idea. The consequences always seemed to be tragic, leaving somebody else behind to clean up the mess.

The street they were on was nicknamed crack

alley and law enforcement patrolled it infrequently in order to keep the drugs and bad behavior contained to one area. It was easier for them if they just left that one small part of town alone.

On the upside, a fire like this was a stoner's dream come true. It was one badass bonfire that gave new meaning to high on hash.

On the downside, it was a dangerous fire to fight. Too many dim-witted people to worry about. Instead of running from the fire, the idiots were drawn to it. Going after one big rush without realizing they might get burned.

Someday soon the entire neighborhood would be toast and developers could finally make their own dreams come true.

Like every other time since Tanner started at the firehouse, Emmitt and Tanner teamed up, the cadet tethered to the teacher.

Being alone in somebody else's house, having none of his own crap, made the day drag by for Skye. There was nothing for him to do but fiddle around and make the best of what was there. Reading Firefighter's Digest wasn't really of much interest to him, though the guys pictured in it were nice to look at, he finished paging through the mag in five minutes. A few cocktails and a lap in the pool helped him pass the time slightly faster than watching the grass grow.

He thought the evening would never arrive, but like every day, it did. The sun eventually set, the moon finally rose and he had no communication with Tanner throughout the day. Skye had no right to claim the guy, but it drove him crazy not having heard from him at all. He knew Tanner had a job to do, but couldn't help wondering if the guy was okay or not. He thought many times about calling Tanner, but decided against it because it wasn't part of their deal: yet. Tanner had his life and Skye had his. He was Tanner's guest, not a live-in love interest.

Times are changing, though. So Skye thought, too bad, enough waiting. The guy left in a raging fire engine so Skye had every right to worry, boyfriend or not. Anybody in their right mind would be concerned.

Skye lay in the poolside lounge chair, picked up his cell phone, and touched the text message icon instead of calling. The odds of Tanner answering his phone would be slim, so he sent a short text that just said *how was your day?*

Skye waited a while, kept watching for his phone to light up, but nothing came through from Tanner. No reply or even a note that bounced back mentioning the message had been read. Nothing.

Thirty minutes later, still no reply. Skye sent another text that said, *hope all is well.*

Thirty more minutes passed with no reply. At this point, Skye was worried. He got up and paced the backyard, walking from one end of the pool to the other, chewing a fingernail until it hurt.

ৎ   ৶

On the way back to the fire station after dousing the bonfire that put smiles on so many faces, another call came in that detoured the truck and its crew.

A firefighter's job was more than turning a hot blaze into smoldering ashes or helping a cat out of a tree. That was all in the past. These days a fireman did more than just handle his hose.

Pressing nine-one-one didn't always mean there was a fire.

This particular call was one of those times. No fire or smoke. It was an automobile rollover along the highway. A speeding SUV bounced off a bigger truck during an attempt at a fancy pass and ended up on its side in a ditch.

As usual, traffic slowed way down, bringing the fire truck to a crawl. If it weren't for so many rubber-neckers in passing cars, the fire truck would've gotten to the accident much faster.

When the crew reached the scene of the rollover, there were police cars already stacked up that forced the oncoming traffic to the far left lane, making room for the rescue teams.

Tanner and Emmitt were the first out of the cab and on their way across the field to where the SUV was lying on its side.

In the driver's seat was a kid in his late teens or early twenties, on the verge of hysteria because he couldn't free himself from the safety belt or open up the door.

While Emmitt tried to calm the kid down, Tanner hit the underside of the vehicle with an extinguisher in case a stray spark decided it needed to become a flame.

Because the door had been dented and jammed, getting it open by hand alone was not going to happen. Tools to break the door away were needed.

While Tanner went for the tools, Emmitt talked to the kid, asking if he was hurt.

The kid stuck behind the steering wheel was freaking out. Intermingled with hysterical screaming and some tears, he kept repeating, "Help me out of here, please."

Emmitt assured the kid they would.

Tanner made it back to the SUV with a metal bending apparatus, climbed up next to Emmitt and handed it to him. Peering into the driver's side window, Tanner saw fear crumpling the kid's face as if Tanner was the reaper staring down at him.

Working as a team, Emmitt and Tanner fastened the jaws between the door and the car frame, twisted the crank until the hinges cracked and the door was able to be pulled away and tossed to the ground. Together, Tanner and Emmitt pulled the kid out and turned him over to the EMT to be examined.

"Good job again, cadet," Emmitt said, kicking the door aside. "Soon you'll be the Cap."

"Thanks, Emm. Gotta make lieutenant first." Tanner picked up the jaws and carried them back to the truck.

"I see potential."

"Thanks again, Emm."

"Hey, Tan. About that guy we fixed up yesterday. Are you and him hooking up?" Emmitt asked. "What's the deal with that?"

"It's a possibility," Tanner answered.

"Oh shit. I screwed that up for you didn't I? Sorry, man."

"You didn't screw anything up."

"It sure looked like I did. If I'd known you were making a move on the guy, I never would've gone looking for you in the garage." Emmitt slammed the truck's tool compartment shut.

"It was hardly a move, just a mating dance." Tanner thought about what it could have been.

"Come on, don't be coy. I saw you going in for the kill."

Tanner pulled off his coat and jumped into the fire truck cab. "Kiss my ass."

"I'll leave that up to your new boyfriend. He's probably better at it than I would ever be." Emmitt pushed the gearshift into drive and they drove away.

"I hope so." Tanner laughed.

Chapter 8

Skye told himself to hell with it, and went ahead and made that call, the one that would hopefully confirm that Tanner was okay. He hated the feeling of not knowing. When the phone buzzed on the other end of Skye's ear, somebody other than Tanner picked it up. For an instant, panic lassoed Skye before he had a chance to say anything.

"Hello," the sleepy voice said.

Skye pulled the phone away from his ear and looked at it, making sure Tanner's name was displayed. It was, so he returned it to his head and then said, "Hi, is Tanner around and may I speak to him?"

The tired voice yawned. "Um... I think he's out on a run. Hang on, I'll go check."

Skye worried painfully while waiting for an answer, at the same time ranting, "C'mon, c'mon, c'mon."

He gripped his elbow to aid in holding the

phone to the ear he could feel getting redder with every second that ticked by. Skye was a worrier, had been all his life. He'd been told almost daily not to sweat the small stuff, don't worry about it until it happened; but he still did.

To Skye, not being able to reach Tanner was good enough reason to worry. How could he not? The guy was probably in a burning building dodging flames.

Finally the voice returned to the phone, a little more rejuvenated but still dragging his words as if he'd been drinking the night before. "He's not here but I can tell him you called. Who is this?"

Skye exhaled, holding a hand against his chest and told the guy on the line, "Please let him know Skye called."

"Yeah, sure. I'm writing it down now." Another yawn and the phone went quiet.

"Wait. My number," Skye hollered, but the phone was already silent.

A few minutes after Skye hung up his phone, it rang. The display read Tanner. Skye grabbed it quickly and answered, "Thank God, hello."

It wasn't Tanner on the other end but the yawner who said, "Just checking to make sure I got your number. You just called, right?"

Being kind to the guy, Skye just answered, "Yeah it's me, Skye."

"Cool. I'll tell Tanner you called." Again the phone went silent when whoever was on the other end hung it up.

Skye let out a weak chuckle, expecting a firefighter to be brighter than the guy who answered Tanner's phone, but he supposed it took all kinds to douse a flame. Every vegetable is important in a full-flavored stew, even the small potato. Maybe the guy cleaned the place or washed the trucks, perhaps maintained the lawn. Whoever he was, Skye was sure the man helped complete the station.

"Now what?" Skye picked up the phone that had suddenly displayed Tanner's name again.

"You rang?" Tanner's deep voice was there.

"Oh, shit. Hello." Skye sprang from the lounge so quickly he stubbed his toe on the foot of the chair. He hobbled, wincing, holding his throbbing injury while trying to recover what he just said.

"What?" Tanner questioned with a laugh.

"I thought... Hello there... It's you... Um. Thank God. How are you?" The words sputtered out of Skye's mouth. His tone quickly and coolly lowered when he heard it was Tanner calling and not the guy with the tired voice he thought was calling back again. Hanging onto his reddening toe, he breathed slowly, puffing a few times, trying desperately to conceal his pain from Tanner and act like everything was normal. It wasn't an easy task at the moment but he pulled it off, with rising silence.

Tanner followed Skye's unspoken line of thought, making an effort to pick up on what he was holding back. Tanner cocked his head, heightening his senses in order to hear what was going on in the background and then said, "Are you alright? Where are you?"

With the ache in his toe subsiding, Skye's tone changed again, this time sounding rational.

"I'm hanging out at your house, not doing much except drinking, lounging by the pool and worrying about you."

"I'm fine and always will be, so you can stop stressing over me." Tanner smiled at the idea that somebody was concerned for his welfare.

"If there's one thing I can't do, it's that. Now that I've met you, there's no turning back. I'm hooked and I'm going to worry." When Skye finished speaking, he might have been blushing. Actually, he was; both ears were burning beet red, he could feel it.

A voice inside Tanner's head echoed, *that's sweet*, and then he added, out loud, "I'll be there tomorrow evening, so feel free to make yourself at home. We can do something together then, okay."

Hearing that, Skye beamed, and for the next few seconds he struggled in vain to convey what was on his mind, but his tongue was tied in a knot and his brain felt as though it was asleep. He couldn't spit anything out, just gazed into the empty space in front of him. Finally everything inside him unraveled and he was able to reply, "Tomorrow is good for me. I'll be here, of course."

"See you then." Tanner just about did the happy dance, but that meant he needed to be keen on the house brothers ridiculing and harassing him for the next few weeks for doing it. Eventually somebody else would do something stupider and take the spotlight off him. That's how it worked in the house, no getting away from it.

Chapter 9

Five minutes after Tanner hung up from talking to Skye, he met Emmitt in the locker room where they would rinse and rejuvenate after the long day of events they'd just had. As usual, they were always the last ones lingering in the locker room.

They put on the station blues, prepared for the next call if one came. Tanner's fitted tee accentuated his well-developed form, which sharpened his worn out, but comfy faded blue jeans. He stepped in front of the mirror to inspect himself, standing a moment without moving. A sigh escaped him as he stared.

Emmitt approached Tanner from behind and said, "If you stand in front of that mirror much longer, that image of yours will jump out and take your place."

Tilting his head, Tanner's gaze reflected back at Emmitt.

Switching to Tanner's side, Emmitt snaked

his arm over his shoulder and gave it a light squeeze. He could tell what Tanner was thinking and reassured him by saying, "There's no need to be concerned about the way you look, my friend. You're just fine and I'm pretty sure the guy will like you just the way you are. Now get rid of that sad-ass mug and put on a big-ass smile."

They stood side-by-side, both staring blankly at their reflections in the fogged up mirror.

Tanner expelled a disturbed sigh and said, "I think I've finally met somebody who might be good for me, but I'm afraid of screwing things up. It's only been a day and I've already run out on him."

"You had no choice; you had to go to work. I'm sure he understands and I got the impression he already likes you as you are, and the baggage you drag with you." Emmitt rotated toward Tanner to roll the sleeve up on his right arm to expose the tattoo that decorated his shoulder, pulling it tight to show off his bicep. Then Emmitt helped him roll up the other sleeve, so he appeared balanced.

Tanner asked, "You think so?"

"Certain."

"You sure about that?" Tanner cackled.

"Pretty sure." Emmitt ended the banter with a kiss to the side his friend's brow, turned Tanner's body toward the exit sign and gave him a swat on the ass.

"I'm letting him stay at my place until he has a chance to get back on his feet. He has nowhere else to go right now. We'll see if he's still there tomorrow when I get home," Tanner said.

Emmitt faced Tanner. "You're really fixated

on this guy aren't you?"

"I know it's crazy, but I am. I can't stop thinking about him. I hardly know the guy but my head keeps telling me to go after him, claim his ass and mark it as mine. He's so fucking hot, which makes me want him even more. His burns and all."

Finding it funny how Tanner could be so infatuated with another man, Emmitt laughed at his enthusiasm through pinched lips, spitting some.

"Don't start poking fun at me, you hideous creature." Tanner's forehead wrinkled before his outburst changed to a more genuine tone. "Seriously Emm, Skye is fucking gorgeous. Far be it from me to proclaim love at first sight exists, but I think my thoughts on that just might be leaning toward believing."

Emmitt was thrilled for Tanner. Until Tanner had explained how much he liked Skye, his voice and expression loaded with enthusiasm, Emmitt hadn't realized two men could hit it off in such a major way. He found Tanner's reaction endearing. For the first time since Emmitt met Tanner, he was finally getting to witness his true affection for another man. It was new to Emmitt, but he wanted Tanner to be happy, to find companionship with someone who really mattered to him.

Tanner interrupted Emmitt's racing thoughts with a shoulder to shoulder bump and then completely ruined the serious moment when he said, "Make me something to eat, I'm starving."

"Is there a frying pan in my hand? Do I look like Skye to you? Where is he when *you* need him?"

߷ ߷

Home alone at Tanner's place Skye had a sudden urge to bathe. The salty water in the pool felt good on his skin, but wasn't as refreshing as he would have liked. While he waited for the cascading water in the upstairs shower to reach a temperature tolerable to his burns, he removed the flimsy sports shorts he was wearing. Fully nude, he rotated the handle toward the cold side, bringing the boil down to a cooler level so it didn't make his burns worse.

Standing motionless under the relaxing downpour, Skye warbled a gratifying moan, soaking in the pleasurable massage from the barrage of droplets. Soap in hand, he circled it continually over his chest, until the frothy lather there was trickling to his feet.

Putting the image of Tanner front and center in his mind, he moved his hand to his rising erection, seizing himself in his slippery clutch. He gently stroked himself with a tightened fist, sliding back and forth over his hardened cock. His other hand roamed free, scaling the mounds of his bulky chest, prompting his erection to expand and break his grip. His body tensed as his anxiety rose with an orgasmic frenzy building in his groin. He trembled, gasping for air, relishing the thought of Tanner's pucker wrapped around him, pulling him in. With his eyes closed, he damn near felt Tanner with him, on him, holding him, but before Skye fired his pearly essence across the shower stall, he released his grip, saving what was inside of him for Tanner, the man he wanted to give himself to.

Skye panted, leaned his back against the wet

tiled wall and pulled his hands off his fevered body. Out of breath and gasping, he rinsed himself clean while the swelling between his legs slowly subsided. "Fuckin' A, I want that man."

Stepping from the shower, he dried and then wrapped a white fluffy towel around his waist. Standing in front of the bathroom mirror, he inspected his torso; the ripples down his abdomen and the bulges on his chest.

With nothing of his own to wear, Skye raided Tanner's closet. As respectfully as he could, he nearly mauled every item he saw before deciding on a simple pair of workout shorts, leaving his chest bare.

Skye went back to the pool, dropped into the lounge chair, taking in the sky above him. He looked out over the trees as the sun started setting, rays stretching across the sky, painting the clouds with orange and lavender hues.

Chapter 10

The station was quiet throughout the night, and the last few hours of Tanner's time there seemed to have stalled. With nothing taking place to distract him, Tanner could only think about Skye the entire time, which made him antsy to get home to see him.

It was close to four o'clock p.m., which was the end of his scheduled shift and time for a crew change.

Tanner packed his belongings into his overnight bag, items he carried back and forth with him every time. Just a few of his favorite things, the ones he couldn't seem to live without.

On his way home, he heard a song on the radio he'd always liked and lo and behold, it seemed appropriate at the time. He smiled and sang along to *'Can't Fight Fate.'*

It felt like him meeting Skye was fate. It wasn't planned, or forced, it just happened.

ဖြ ‌ஜ

At the house, Skye paced the floors, sipped wine, and peeked out windows while waiting for Tanner to return home. Antsy wasn't a powerful enough word for how he was feeling about being with Tanner again. Nervous maybe, but most of all he was excited about seeing the good-looking, kind-hearted man who saved his life.

"More wine. I need more wine." Skye shuffled into the kitchen where he left the bottle, open and breathing.

There was no way to mistake what Skye saw when he lifted his head for something he was imagining. He caught site of Tanner standing in the doorway holding a fresh market bag in one hand and a bottle of wine in the other, looking like he had a plan. One that Skye hoped involved himself and a sexual attack to celebrate his recently saved life. He was ready either way.

When Tanner entered the kitchen, relief spread across Skye's face. Tanner's skin-tight T-shirt showed off every hill and gutter running up and down his abs and the bulky mounds of his chest. Skye's spirit immediately lightened and he forgot all about his current situation, the one of being homeless. Even the sting in his side and forearm went away when he saw Tanner there, in the same room as him.

For several moments, Tanner just stood and stared at Skye, running his eyes over every part of him, not missing a thing; as if he were memorizing Skye's beautiful bare chest and perfect torso. And the ivy tattoo was so hot on Skye, he loved it, loved it a lot. Since the first time he saw Skye in his choo-choo night-pants, he'd wanted to get closer to him, run his hands across his chest, over his abs, and take a chance on kissing him.

Skye stepped forward and joined Tanner, standing so close that their body heat was being exchanged.

Resisting temptation, Tanner pushed against Skye, forcing him further into the kitchen. As he did, he swung the grocery bag onto the island countertop and went in for the kiss he'd missed out on yesterday at the station.

Tanner fell back, landing on his elbows against the counter when Skye spun him around and dove into the kiss. Their tongues tangled, wrapped around each other, playing and dancing. A sweet tender kiss it wasn't, but a greedy, lustful one that seemed long overdue.

Skye gripped Tanner's jaw, overpowering and pressing down on him. Not letting up, Skye's tongue hammered inside Tanner's mouth, passionately mashing, transferring desire, spit and lust.

Breathless, Skye rose, pulling Tanner with him. They recklessly spun again, trading places.

Skye fell back against the pantry door with Tanner pushing into him, their heaving chests bumping together, hearts pounding like tympani in an orchestra.

Skye's lust escalated, his arms dangled at his sides, body hanging limp. He shuddered, and then surrendered, quickly hardening beneath his borrowed shorts.

Tanner locked Skye in place against the door

with a tight kiss, holding him there with his body, preventing him from slumping to the floor. He clutched Skye's hands, fanned his arms upward against the door and locked them in place above his head. Remaining lip-locked, Tanner inhaled Skye's breath into his own lungs before slowly dragging his mouth along Skye's cheek to his ear and softly whispering, "That was way overdue." He nipped Skye's earlobe with his tender lips.

Skye's ear burned when Tanner's words vibrated into it. The heat from Tanner's deep voice was apparently subconsciously linked to his cock, making it spring to attention the second he heard those words.

"You're so damned hot," Tanner whispered, then pulled away. "Whatever's in your pocket, I'm impressed."

"Ho—lee—shit! That was the greatest...," Skye slurred. He couldn't even finish.

"If you enjoyed that, wait 'til next time, stud," Tanner added, flicking Skye's chin with his finger.

Skye blinked several times until his senses returned. "That was one of the best kisses I've ever had and it needs to happen again, even if I have to fucking beg you."

"It will. I promise," Tanner assured him.

"If that's any indication of other hidden talents, far be it from me to stop you from making another move."

Tanner grinned. "All you have to do is ask."

"You're going to make me ask?"

"I'm sure it won't come to that because you're too damned irresistible and I'll have a hard time waiting for an invitation." Tanner hesitated a second before adding, "You have my permission to pounce on me any time you want. I wouldn't think of stopping you."

"It's not fair to be teasing me like that." Skye fanned himself.

"It gets much better," Tanner let on.

"Okay, you need to stop talking before I have at you here on the kitchen floor. What do you have to drink? I need a cool-down. Straightaway." Pushing Tanner aside, Skye turned to the refrigerator for a beer. "You want one?"

"I'll take whatever you have to offer." Tanner grinned and took the beer.

Chapter 11

Skye wiped his hands down his chest as if brushing away toast crumbs that landed there during breakfast and said, "I should put a shirt on, don't you think?" He started to walk toward the stairs.

Before Skye had a chance to get away, Tanner grabbed his arm and said, "Don't you dare get dressed. You're good the way you are."

Skye was charmed by Tanner's efforts to keep his shirt off. Not wearing it was fine with him, because he hated shirts, especially the ones that buttoned all the way down the front. They felt stiff and scratchy, over-starched and always felt like they were trying to saw his head off at the neck. If it weren't for needing to wear a shirt for work, he'd never put one on. When he did, he figured why fuss with a button-down when pulling one over his head was so much quicker; also safer for his neck! The many cotton T-shirts he owned were much more comfortable and they didn't need to be ironed before every wearing. A total waste of his time. Stretch one over his bulky chest and he was good to go. Skye generally didn't understand the importance of clothing, unless an event required a certain wardrobe. Once at home, he took it off immediately. Now that he knew Tanner wanted him shirtless, he had even more reason to rip it off every chance he got.

Tugging on Tanner's shirt at the waist, Skye said, "If I'm to be shirtless, then you should be too."

"But I'm shy," Tanner revealed.

"Not possible. With a body like yours, there's no reason to be shy." Skye placed a palm to Tanner's chest, fanning his fingers, sneaking a quick grope that he felt clear through to his bones.

During the time it took Skye to pull his hand from Tanner's chest and reach for his glass of wine, Tanner crazily lifted the bottom hem of his own shirt. He pulled it through the front of the shirt's neck; making a knot at his chest and turning his T-shirt into a halter top, which exposed his deeply cut abs. He laughed about it when Skye turned back around and saw what he'd done.

Skye's eyes zeroed in on Tanner's six-pack abs and he blurted out, "Holy crap, you're ripped." After that he chuckled and said, "Damn nice."

Tanner looked down at himself and laughed at Skye's wide-eyed expression.

Skye refocused, held up his wine glass and asked, "You want a sip?"

"After I finish my beer." Tanner wrapped two fingers around the bottleneck and tossed his head back to swallow a mouthful of malt, the chill rushing his throat was perfection.

Skye watched him drink and confirmed, "You're butch." Skye didn't mind beer, but he preferred wine. Red wine. Shiraz was his favorite, just like it was Tanner's. He pulled another glass from the cabinet, filled it halfway with wine, and pushed it toward Tanner. He added more to his own glass to make them even.

They'd been in the kitchen for about an hour and the bag Tanner brought with him hadn't been touched; Skye hadn't even looked to see what was in it. They were too busy getting to know each other to be digging into a little brown bag.

Skye leaned into the counter with his hands folded around the bell of the wine glass and asked, "Are we sticking around?"

At that moment Tanner glanced up, his face lighting up when he saw Skye's eyes meet his with his sexiest look. Tanner started to smile, and then stopped himself. His mouth opened. Closed. He squirmed and tried to relax. Taking a sip of wine helped. He smiled again, this time it stayed. "I was thinking about going out, showing you off, but I'd rather keep you all to myself in the privacy of our own home. Uh-oh, is it too soon to call it ours?"

For a moment Skye disconnected from his surroundings, then turned his attention back to Tanner, and kept his answer short, "Good idea."

Tanner noticed hesitation and asked, "What's wrong?"

"It's my burns," Skye answered with a crumpled brow. "Maybe I should take this off and let the air get at it." He pointed to his bandaged waist.

Tanner didn't agree. "Not a good idea, it needs to stay clean or it could get infected. We should probably change the wrap, though. Let's get the pain relieving ointment to help soothe it."

The problem with pain was that it seemed to show up at the worst times. Like this time, when the get-to-know-each-other-better gropes and feels were about to get underway.

Skye grunted when he moved, but followed through with the doctor's orders and went upstairs to apply fresh gauze with Tanner's help, since he knew more about dressing burns than Skye did.

It only took a few minutes for Tanner to fix Skye up, and when he was done, he stood and gave Skye a gentle kiss on the lips. It was a compassionate one, lasting several moments and it took Skye's breath away. Pain or no pain, stiffness rose in both of them. That was inevitable.

Considering Skye's current condition, they decided to disentangle from each other and let their erections rest. It was best to take it easy on their first night together, instead of getting all riled up and aggravating his still-fresh wounds. It was going to be tough, but keeping their boners to themselves was a done deal. For the time being.

They also decided to stay at the house instead of going out somewhere. It was the better of the two choices, and that way Tanner could keep Skye shirtless like he wanted.

Chapter 12

After finishing their grilled chicken dinner on the back sundeck, Skye and Tanner took advantage of their quiet surroundings, sitting side by side on a settee by the pool, relaxing while looking up and counting stars. It was getting late, but neither of them cared.

Tanner opened his hand on top of Skye's thigh, inviting him to take it.

Glancing at Tanner's upturned palm, then switching his gaze to meet his eyes, Skye slid his hand into Tanner's. He became hypnotized when Tanner's touch alone made his heart turn warm.

As hard as he tried, Tanner could no longer contain his obsession. He abruptly rolled into Skye's body, putting them face to face without moving from the settee.

Tanner pulled Skye to him, cradling his body next to his own. Their hearts beat rhythmically, pounding faster. They held each other's gaze until their lust grew too strong. They each lunged for the other, hearts pounding, lungs sucking air while they feverishly kissed.

Several minutes passed before Tanner eased back, bringing a hand to Skye's chest, enraptured by its muscled splendor. Before letting another minute go by, Tanner slid his hand upward, lightly resting it on the nape of Skye's neck, caressing and gently twisting his fingers in his hair.

Skye trembled when Tanner touched him. His head gradually fell back, forcing his eyes to thin slits.

Tanner leaned forward, his warm chest tightly pressed against Skye's. Caringly placing his mouth to Skye's, he softly kissed him. Their heads leisurely moved from side to side, tongues greeting one another romantically.

Withdrawing smoothly, Tanner tilted his head and whispered; "Now that was a kiss to remember." His hand still lay fanned on Skye's chest, feeling it rise and fall with every breath.

Skye spoke cautiously, keeping his voice low. "That it was. But maybe we should slow down before your neighbors catch us."

A sneaky wind gust pushed them back together as if pointing out Skye's worries to be unfounded.

Dousing that thought as well, Tanner warmly kissed Skye again. His wet tongue then traced Skye's lips before the kiss had a chance to end.

Skye shyly pulled away. He wasn't the type to put his affection for another man on display in public. He wasn't ready for that, and wasn't sure if he ever would be.

Tanner however was okay with it. He didn't

seem to care if anyone saw him for who he was. He was proud of it, of himself, and who he was with. Kissing a man in an open grove was as natural to him as breathing was and the opinions of others had no bearing on his behavior. Though what Skye said stung straight to his bones, thinking it had more to do with himself than it did Skye, Tanner chose to let it go. "How about we take this inside?" he suggested.

Even with his reservations about the neighborhood watching, Skye stood, still holding Tanner's hand, leading the way back into the house.

They spent a good hour in the kitchen, chitchatting and cleaning up the mess they made during dinner preparations, doing their best to impress each other. It was the time for that; fluff the feathers and puff up that chest. Unlike the first time they were in the kitchen, a few sweet kisses were exchanged. Nothing intense like before.

Polishing the granite counter with a rag right after another kiss, or rather, a peck, Tanner said, "Do you hunt?"

"What? Hunt?" Skye squawked, oddly surprised.

"Yeah—Do you hunt?"

"No, I don't hunt. That's a strange question to ask after a peck on the cheek."

"Okay, then. Do you fish?" Tanner continued.

"No." Skye's brow knotted and he sent Tanner a glance of dismay. "This is getting weird. What's going on? Is this your way of figuring out my place on the macho-scale?"

Tanner sniggered. "Not at all. Just wondering what's in store for me."

"I'm not a lesbian, if that's what you're getting at. If you're into lesbians, I know a few who love to fish and hunt. I could introduce you to them," Skye joked.

Laughing at what Skye said, Tanner replied, "Okay, glad you're not a lesbian, not that there's anything wrong with that, but I want to know how things with you work."

"Didn't you have that figured out while I was crushing you on this countertop and then when you had me up against the pantry door?" Skye looked crossly at Tanner.

With a crooked smirk Tanner said, "Well actually I had some idea — sort of figured it out when you pushed me back against the granite to kiss me and the way you took my kiss against the door."

"Everything was okay with that, right?"

"Absolutely. It was perfect."

"Which really means?" Skye lowered his head.

"That means we probably fit together quite well. I fit you and you fit me." Tanner waggled his brow.

Skye shook his head, but followed it with a grin. "Now that we have that cleared up, I'm just going to be blunt with you. No riddles to figure out."

Tanner leaned in, anticipating what Skye had to say.

Skye's expression changed to a more positive one. "I'd prefer to spend most of my time under you, meaning I consider myself a bottom more than a top, although pretty damn good at both. I'm guessing you are too, which means to me that we *should* fit together in any situation. Top. Bottom. Pitcher. Catcher. Giver. Receiver. Whatever," he said with a smile.

Tanner grinned and said, "Beautifully put. Time for bed."

Chapter 13

Going to bed sexually frustrated was never an easy thing for a horny man. It turned out to be a long night for Tanner and Skye; both experiencing blue balls after the conversation in the kitchen. One slept upstairs and the other down.

For Skye, the strain of an unrelenting erection was more than he could bear, which prompted his hand to move down and grip the beast. Thanks to Tanner's good looks, charm and rocking hot body, it only took a few strokes to release the built up tension between his legs, semen pelting his chest and face.

On the lower level, the same sexual frustration dominated Tanner's thoughts. Lying in the dark, thinking of Skye, he jacked his thick erection with a lubricated fist. Within minutes of getting started, he flooded his torso and chest with pent up spunk while wishing Skye was there with him to take it all in.

After cumming alone, both reached a state of

satisfied relaxation, and were able to slumber until morning.

Throughout the night, each was bombarded by dreams of the other causing erections that out-lasted any they'd ever had before. The intensity of their dream-induced hard-ons could punch holes through steel.

Too anxious to sleep late, because the anticipation of seeing Skye again wouldn't let him rest, Tanner woke well before the sun. Springing out of bed, he hit the shower to clean the sleep away. He sang while the water from the showerhead poured over his naked body. His voice cracked a few times when he reached for the high notes, but he went on singing anyway.

When he felt fresh enough, Tanner stepped from the shower. He wrapped a towel around his waist, snagging another one to pat the water drops from his face and chest, before taking off to the kitchen to pour a cup of black magic.

Back in front of his closet, Tanner snapped the towel from around his waist and tossed it recklessly into the hamper next to the door. Standing naked, he picked out a pair of boxer briefs, a white fitted T-shirt, and a pair of navy cargo shorts and put them all on.

In a good mood because of the way Skye made him feel, Tanner went back to the kitchen, held his coffee cup with both hands and waited for his hot new beau to show.

Dressed in office attire, Skye met Tanner in the kitchen and said, "Good morning, sunshine."

"Wow. You look nice. Someplace to go?" Tanner handed Skye a cup of coffee.

"I need this. Thank you." Skye took the cup, blowing at the steam rising above it. "I told the office I'd be in today. Life must go on."

"Where'd you get the shirt and pants?" Tanner asked.

"After the taxi took me to get my car, I stopped off at the store and picked them up; along with a few other things I might need," Skye said.

"Smart." Tanner was disappointed about Skye having to work, and surprised that he hadn't mentioned it before. "You gonna be gone all day?"

"Mostly, I'm afraid."

"You coming back?" Tanner tried to keep the regret out of his voice.

"If that's okay with you."

"Of course it is. I want you to."

"Then I'll see you later." Skye winked.

"I'll be waiting." Tanner kissed him.

Chapter 14

Something didn't seem right with the picture. Three days ago, Skye had a home to call his own, which contained everything he needed. Then, just like that, he was homeless. With only a car and a few burns to serve as a reminder of how quickly his life had changed. Was the change for better or for worse? Even with Tanner added to the newer picture, Skye wasn't sure about the answer.

At the office that morning, while Skye sat at his desk, kicking back and wondering what his next project at the agency was going to be, his boss walked in with a box.

Staggered by the unusual entry, Skye sat upright and then quickly stood and asked, "Did something change while I was away?"

His boss set the box on Skye's mechanical drawing table and laid out notes and folders like he was a fisherman dumping the catches of the day on Pelican Bay's wharf. "Get over here," he ordered.

Skye stepped to the table, and for what

seemed like a full minute, his boss stared directly into his eyes.

Finally making a move, his boss tossed the box aside, grabbed Skye by the shoulders, and said, "Glad you're alright kid. We've been worried about you. How's everything?" Then he hugged Skye, digging his short scruffy beard into Skye's neck.

"I'm good, but you scared me with that box, Jack. I thought you were firing my ass and that was all you were giving me to take my junk out of here." Skye's tone changed from nervous shaking to calm and collected.

Jack let go of Skye and turned to the table. He spread out what he'd just poured from the box so they could get a look at everything with a few quick glances. "Nonsense. We've got a major project to bid on and you're the only one I have confidence in to lead the team."

"I appreciate that, Jack. What is it?"

"A mid-rise on the Upper Northside, nineteen stories, office spaces, and retail shops located on the ground level. Above that, residential; apartments first, and then condos will take over the top five floors."

"Sounds great. When do we meet with the developers?" Skye picked up a folder and looked through it. There wasn't much there, but first files never filled out until the initial meeting took place.

"Tomorrow morning is our big moment. They're coming to us, which is a positive sign. We need to be ready." Jack started backing out the door then added, "Everything's good with you right, Skye?"

"Yeah—Yeah... Good." Skye looked at his

feet and then up at Jack.

Jack could tell something had changed in Skye, and it didn't appear to be a fire related thing.

Skye did it again: looked down and then up. "I'd like to tell you something, Jack."

"Aw shit, Skye, what have you done?" Jack grimaced.

"I haven't done anything, Jack. I'd just like to fill you in on what's happened in the past couple of days." Skye's voice went lower.

"Go ahead. What is it?" Jack stopped in the doorway before taking a few hesitant steps back inside Skye's office.

After seeing Jack's face go long, Skye quickly discarded what he was initially going to say. "Well, as you know I'm sort of homeless. So if you know of any nice apartments with reputable landlords available, let me know."

"Okay, that's a relief. I thought you were going to tell me you lit the fire in your apartment as an easy way out. I know it wasn't in the best part of town." Jack paced the floor.

"You crazy ass, you'd better be joking. Walking away from my lease would have been better than arson." Skye flipped Jack the proverbial fuck-you finger.

Jack raised his hands in surrender and said, "Just making sure, and what did I tell you about that finger?"

"It's like my trademark farewell salute to you. It suits you." Skye laughed.

"I appreciate that you always let me see it. Most everybody else waits until I leave the room." Jack turned to walk away.

Skye's finger jokingly went up again.

"I felt that," Jack grumbled. "You're an ass."

Jack turned back around and asked, "Wait a minute. What do you mean 'sort of homeless?' Are you living in your car?"

After taking a deep breath, Skye answered, "No—no, one of the firemen who helped me out of the building hooked me up with a temporary place."

"That was good of him," Jack said apprehensively and then walked away.

Skye wanted to say more to Jack, but for many reasons, his head kept telling him not to. After recent events, which could have ended tragically for Skye, he realized how short life was and that it could be whisked away in a matter of seconds. He'd come close to being one of those statistics a few days earlier. When his apartment turned to ash with him in it, he would have, if Tanner hadn't been there. Skye had always been upfront with Jack about most things. The exception being one important detail which he kept personal; that he was gay.

Since Skye had met Tanner, the impulse to share the news was mounting, but he still couldn't let it out, not even to Jack. Skye wasn't ashamed for being attracted to other men, he was just afraid to lose a close friend because of being gay. He had witnessed the way people reacted to hearing that news. Those experiences made him want to be far away from the side of the battle that sometimes took the bullets: the side of the person revealing their sexuality. It was easier to stay quiet. Other than his father, Skye hadn't allowed many people in on that part of his life; his gay life, but with Tanner in it now, he had the urge to open up to those close to him.

Chapter 15

That evening, after Skye's first day back at the office, he returned to Tanner's house at the unheard hour of seven p.m., dragging ass.

Already at home, with simple plans to watch the sky go black on that July night; Tanner set two stemmed glasses and a pricey bottle of Merlot out on the kitchen counter. Hearing the car door slam, Tanner went to meet Skye at the front door with a grin on his face so big it looked like the sun was still shining. "It's about time you got here." He stood with his back against the inside frame of the doorway.

"I'm happy to see you, too," Skye said, and then kissed Tanner's cheek when he passed him.

"The cheek? That's all I get?" Tanner furrowed his brow, crossed his arms across his shirtless chest, and followed Skye into the kitchen.

Skye collapsed into Tanner's chest and offered a guarantee. "There's more. But I'd like to get out of this scratchy shirt before it hacks my head off at the neck." Skye tugged at the stiff collar while thoroughly kissing Tanner. "Was that one better?"

Tanner nodded while eagerly helping Skye unbutton the offending shirt and peeling it back over his shoulders. He got his lips back over Skye's immediately.

"Damn, you're beautiful. Do you know that?" Tanner whispered into his mouth.

Skye pulled his arms from the sleeves and tossed the shirt to the floor, giving Tanner the access to his bare chest Skye knew he wanted.

Tanner burned inside as he ran his open hands across Skye's chest, thinking how much he wanted to be with him. Just Skye. Nobody else.

As their kiss lingered, it became clear to Tanner how much Skye wanted him, too. Their connection was strong; Tanner felt it in the way Skye kissed him back.

Only a few minutes after the kissing started, they found themselves at the door to the back deck. It came as a surprise to both of them; neither of them realized they'd traveled so far, they were so caught up in the kisses.

Skye stumbled over the threshold, breaking their embrace, and he laughed. "Maybe that's a sign we should cool it a second so we can catch our breath," he said, adjusting the erection brought on by Tanner's touch.

Tanner had planned to start the evening outside, anyway. "I'll grab the wine and meet you by the pool," he suggested.

At the shallow end of the pool, Skye rolled up his pant legs, sat contentedly on the edge and waited for Tanner to join him. As he brushed his feet across the pool's floor, each movement pushed ripples away in search of the other side.

Tanner quietly tiptoed around wrought iron furniture until he approached Skye from behind just moments after they had parted.

Engrossed in the dynamics of the moving water, Skye flinched when Tanner reached down and touched his shoulder. Skye rolled his head back and looked up, catching Tanner's smiling gaze. It was a good look on him; one Skye could easily get used to.

After depositing the wine and glasses carefully on the pool's edge, Tanner's hands stroked Skye's collarbone and neck, his gentle touch making Skye's chest expand. After a few minutes, Tanner lowered himself beside Skye and instead of staying seated he stepped into the pool, swam away and went under completely.

With gleaming eyes, Skye watched Tanner disappear beneath the moonstruck surface at the deeper end of the pool.

Tanner reappeared looking like a sodden angel, slicking back his wet hair with his fingers. Tiny moonlit water droplets trickled down his chest as he treaded back to Skye, where he stood between his legs, looking straight at him with a gluttonous gaze.

Unable to resist the man when he was within reach, Skye gripped Tanner's jaw in both hands and kissed him. Pulling back, he said, "You are fucking beautiful, Tanner. Do you know that?"

With lips still connected, Tanner replied, "Glad you think so, but remember who said that first, and to whom."

Remaining locked on Tanner's mouth, Skye pulled him closer until their bare chests met and their confined erections ground together. For a moment it was just the two of them, alone and sharing their budding love. Suddenly Skye withdrew, anxiety stifling his drive to continue what they'd started. He remembered they were in an open place, on display for anybody to see. He couldn't bear the consequences of being seen kissing another man. He pushed against Tanner's chest. "The neighbors. Can they see us?"

Tanner guided Skye back to where he wanted him to be and whispered, "It's alright, Skye, nobody around here cares."

Skye remained frozen in place and gripped the edge of the pool. His body quivered and his abdomen tightened, as tension grew within him.

Tanner observed Skye's anxiety and whispered, "It's okay. We can do this." He pressed his lips to Skye's again, shushing him.

Skye's eyes fluttered when Tanner's kiss intensified. He wanted to get closer to Tanner at the poolside but his fear of being seen overruled his desire. "Would it be alright with you if we took this inside?" Skye asked, defeat clear in his voice. He looked around to see if anyone was watching.

Tanner's heart sank when Skye pushed him away, but he understood. He hadn't been in Skye's position for such a long time; he'd forgotten what it was like to live in fear of the opinions of others. He felt sad for Skye. Being in an ongoing war with himself; feeling the need to hide who he was from everyone. Tanner complied with Skye's wishes.

"Sure, that's fine with me, or we can just sit together out here, sip our wine, count stars and sneak in a kiss when no one's looking," he suggested.

A thankful smile lit up Skye's face as he apologized to Tanner for still having one foot chained to the back wall of the closet.

Tanner lifted his hand to the side of Skye's head, tucking a few loose wisps of hair behind his ear and told him, "Don't you dare apologize. You've done nothing wrong."

"I suppose you're right, but I don't want to be the one taking away your freedom because I'm a chicken shit," Skye said.

Dragging water with him, Tanner sat next to Skye on the edge of the pool. He adjusted himself, took Skye's hand in his, and said, "I can deal with it because I like you, Skye. Couples adjust to each other."

Skye looked at Tanner and tried not to grin after hearing him say the word "couples," like they were one already. He squeezed Tanner's hand, reciprocating the affectionate gesture, not wanting to let go.

While they sat outside sipping wine that evening, Skye shared more details with Tanner than he'd planned to. The deciding factor to let the words come was that he didn't care to keep secrets from Tanner, mostly because he liked him. A lot. He told Tanner about the conversation he'd had with Jack that day. How he'd been seconds from telling him he was gay and that the hunky fireman who'd hooked him up with temporary housing was his boyfriend in the making.

Tanner bumped his shoulder against Skye's; smirked and then said, "Boyfriend in the making, huh? I like that."

"It could happen," Skye confessed.

Tanner needed confirmation. "What could? Telling Jack about you kissing men or getting that boyfriend?"

Skye remained coy. "With any luck, both."

"I see," Tanner said. "Hope the boyfriend part happens first."

"It could, but if things don't work out, I might break his heart," Skye said.

Tanner looked around the yard before he quickly planted a kiss on Skye's cheek and said, "You can break my heart if you want to."

Chapter 16

Skye and Tanner took their mutual lust inside the house to finish that kiss. Starting the second they stepped through the door. It got hotter the further into the kitchen they went, man-handling each other like they hadn't been together in months.

Tanner's instincts told him he wasn't the only one who wanted to fuck or get fucked that night. He was confident, but at the same time hoped his instincts wouldn't backfire. He'd had that happen in the past due to his insatiable sexual appetite. Without brooding about it further, he boldly said, "I can't wait another minute, Skye. I need you in my bed."

Barely registering what Tanner said, Skye reached down and stroked Tanner's hardened cock through his wet shorts, giving tacit approval to his request.

They broke apart and Tanner back-stepped down the hallway to his bedroom. He towed Skye with him by both hands, not breaking their gaze. Once there, Tanner lunged for Skye, taking his kisses and giving back his tongue.

Between the two of them, they wasted no time getting their pants off. Avidly, Skye went for Tanner's zipper, forcing his shorts to his ankles, and in return, Tanner stripped Skye of his work pants. They stood there briefly, totally nude and fully aroused. Muscle against muscle, and cock greeting cock.

Still kissing, Tanner heroically scooped Skye up and threw him on the bed.

Skye bounced on the springy mattress when he landed, every limb rattled before he finally settled on his side, propped on one elbow. He was eager for Tanner to pounce and finish him off like he'd promised.

Cornering his prey, Tanner crawled on all fours until he reached Skye, pushing his shoulder until he was flat on his back. Tanner nipped Skye's lips and whispered, "You ready for a performance you'll never forget?"

Skye lay quietly as Tanner positioned his body on top of him. He shuddered when Tanner's sculpted torso and chest skimmed delicately against his naked flesh. Reaching up, Skye stroked Tanner's chest, absorbing its strength and taking in the beauty.

Tanner leaned down for a kiss, clutched Skye's wrist, and rotated it above his head, holding it there. With his other hand, Tanner caressed Skye's chest, tenderly circling one nub and then flicking harshly at the other.

The touch made Skye's body vibrate, his

words slurred. "I need to feel you, Tanner."

Submitting to Skye's wish without question, Tanner reached to the nightstand where he kept the lube and condoms that would make the connection easier as well as safe. As he did, Skye admired the steam-punk tattoo that formed a shield over his right shoulder and fishtailed down his bicep to his elbow. It moved with him as if the gears were in motion.

Tanner moved back atop Skye, leaned forward and tenderly kissed him.

Skye inhaled sharply when he felt Tanner's oily hand brush across his greedy entrance. His anticipation at the idea of feeling Tanner's cock moving inside him increased.

Sensing how eager Skye was to get fucked, Tanner wrapped and greased his erection in a hurry. But instead of driving it into Skye hard and fast, he took his time entering him. Teasing his opening. Gently tapping at Skye's glistening star with the crest of his oily cock.

Skye's anticipation grew when he felt Tanner's crown breach his hole. He moaned for it, begging to be impaled. His legs spread wide to let Tanner in.

Tanner eased further inside, teasing still, gently moving back and forth until his cock slowly started to disappear.

Euphoria built in Skye with every slow-moving inch he received from Tanner. Skye's abdomen crunched, causing his upper body to jerk violently off the bed. His mouth sprung open when Tanner gave him still more.

With the heat of Skye's channel wrapped

tightly around his dick, Tanner's face softened. He held still to relish the sensation and to prevent himself from cumming too quickly. Skye felt that good surrounding him. Tanner slowly backed almost all the way out of Skye, and then tenderly kissed his lips while gradually gliding his cock back in, slowly inching toward Skye's beating heart.

Skye gasped as the sting of Tanner's intrusion diminished in a matter of seconds, a punishing satisfaction coursing through him, making him moan.

Tanner smoothly rolled his hips, forcing his hard-on deeper, making Skye whimper for it; beg for more. Lowering himself down onto Skye, Tanner trembled, muttering, "You feel amazing, Skye. I could stay inside you forever." He crunched his abs and pushed, reaching the deepest spot he could within Skye, shuddering as Skye's channel massaged and sucked his entire cock in.

Reaching up, Skye clasped both hands to Tanner's jaw. "Look at me, Tanner."

Tanner's eyes met Skye's.

"Please kiss me when you cum," Skye asked sincerely.

Taking his rhythm down to a slower roll, Tanner leaned in and kissed Skye.

Skye pulled Tanner tightly to his chest, kissing him with tenderness, as Tanner eased in and out of him with long, slow strokes. The orgasmic sensation flushed over both of them. Skye's devoted passion instigated a need in Tanner to let go of what he had, pump his churning semen into the man he was penetrating.

They fucked and made love, giving and taking, making sure the other felt fulfilled.

As Tanner dug deeper, his body buffed Skye's torso, holding him within a prolonged orgasmic sensation.

Noticing the extreme pleasure traveling throughout Skye's body, Tanner stilled his rhythm, not letting Skye cum yet. Tanner lay motionless and let Skye's channel impulsively stroke him, naturally craving what he had, trying to take it from him.

Unable to hold back, Tanner dived into Skye's neck with moaning pleasure while resuming the rhythmic rolling of his hips. Tanner picked up his pace, thumping, pounding, and drilling his dick into Skye, urging him to take his cum. He was ready to give Skye all he had.

Skye roared each time Tanner burrowed deep, feeling he had to cum.

Tanner ground his cock into Skye, banging harder, drilling faster as if pounding his image into the bed was his ultimate goal.

Skye's body convulsed as the sensation of his climax increased internally. His insides madly flexed, stroking Tanner's dick like a fisted hand. His tight ring squeezed and tugged, pulling Tanner in, trying to take what his body needed.

Tanner felt Skye's excitement spiraling and knew it was time to let go. Shoving his cock deeper into Skye's ass, he groaned. "Oh fuck, here it comes, Skye." His face knotted from the intense buzz igniting inside him. "Are you ready for me?"

Taking hold of his own dick, Skye nodded. His eyes squeezed shut and his mouth sprung open wide.

Tanner lunged for Skye's mouth, molesting his mug with intense obsession at the same time he powerfully drove his dick in and out of him.

Skye pumped himself, stroking in unison with every one of Tanner's thrusts. He felt Tanner's body go rigid and witnessed his eyes clamp shut.

Pleasured but composed moans escaped Tanner's vocal cords as he continued to hammer Skye; thumping hard until his moaning turned to guttural groans.

Skye trembled, on the edge of his own brimming release.

Collapsing on top of Skye, kissing him with a probing tongue, Tanner's entire body abruptly stiffened. His back arched, forcing his thick cock to the hilt inside Skye. Tanner's hips repeatedly jerked forward as he transferred his white-hot semen into the man he was fucking.

Skye felt Tanner's dick pulsate as it gushed inside him again and again. The sensation pushed Skye to that intense orgasmic moment where every muscle grew taught and his pelvis buzzed.

To heighten Skye's already amazing pleasure, Tanner dug his stiff dick into him harder, prodding, and poking, striking his prostate with the crown of his cock over and over. Tormenting him repeatedly, to enhance Skye's release.

Overflowing with intense ecstasy, Skye's upper body jerked forward off the bed. His hands fastened to Tanner's chest, he let out an aggressive whine along with glistening ribbons of cum that shot from his cock, splashing into the headboard above his head.

Enjoying what was happening under him, Tanner kept drilling Skye; banging his ass, pushing him to shoot more. *Amazing. Fucking amazing,* he thought.

Skye's abdomen crunched, contracting like waves on an ocean, helping his insides squeeze out the last of what remained inside of him. After an extended time shooting cum, the surge within Skye finally ended. He shuddered, taking deep breaths, exhaling with roars before reaching the point where he was able to relax.

Tanner settled his body down against Skye's semen-soaked chest. "That was so fucking hot, I didn't want it to end," he said, breathlessly.

An erratic chuckle came out of Skye, mixed with the twitches and gasps. He wrapped his arms around Tanner's neck and told him, "That *was* hot. Fucking amazing if you want the truth."

Tanner held Skye and kissed him again, lying motionless and staying connected. Many minutes passed before Tanner pulled his cock out of Skye and hid the loaded condom in the towel next to the bed. Repositioning himself tightly against Skye's backside, comfortably beneath the sheets, Tanner spooned him, cradling Skye in his arms.

Tanner whispered into Skye's ear as he held him from behind. "This is the life. This is exactly what we need." His dick turned hard all over again as it pressed perfectly between Skye's ass cheeks, almost going back to the place it just left.

Skye wiggled his hips, backing his body tighter against Tanner, feeling warm and completely satisfied.

Tanner crunched his abdomen one more

time, forcing his swollen dick to snake higher up Skye's spine, where it comfortably rested for the night. Snuggling as close as he could to Skye with one arm wrapped over his shoulder and a palm to his chest, Tanner kissed him below the ear and said, "See you in the morning, hun."

Skye adored how good it felt with Tanner lying next to him in bed. He rotated his head over his shoulder to snatch the last kiss of the night from Tanner's lips. Feeling content, the way he knew he should, Skye exhaled while reaching for Tanner's hand to hold it.

Chapter 17

Six in the morning buzzed on the clock at the same time the sun broke horizon, and the two mixed sources pulled Tanner out of his sleep before Skye awoke. Skye was sleeping face down with one arm draped across Tanner's chest, one leg hooked over his hip, and a raging hard-on digging into his thigh. Getting close and staying that way even during sleep.

Facing the ceiling, Tanner lay with one arm pinned under Skye. He didn't care, having a man sleeping in his arms felt good; especially someone like Skye. Bending his trapped arm at the elbow, Tanner slowly moved his hand to Skye's head and laid it there, gently running strands of his dark umber hair through each curled finger.

The sun squeezed thin beams of light between the open slats in the blinds and the brightness of the rays made Skye stir. He arched his back to stretch, glancing at Tanner with one squinting eye and grumbled, "Good morning, stud."

Kissing the top of Skye's head, Tanner answered back with a "good morning" of his own.

Shifting his hand, Skye moved it from Tanner's chest to his stone-hard cock. "Wow. Perfectly firm." It throbbed, thick and warm in Skye's strained grasp.

Tanner lifted his hips, sliding his dick between Skye's thumb and fingers. "Fuck, your hand feels about as good as your tight ass."

Displaying his gratitude for the compliments, Skye squeezed and stroked Tanner's hot rod, making pre-cum trickle from the slit of his bulbous crown.

"Oh fuck, you've got a gift." Tanner huffed, watching Skye work his magic.

Skye's hand smoothly moved back and forth over Tanner's erection as he moved his mouth closer to it. In a few seconds, the head was going to meet his tongue.

Tanner's body tightened and then he grunted. "Are you trying to make me cum?"

Before Skye had a chance to answer or even slip the head of Tanner's dick into his mouth, he noticed the time. He needed to kick it into turbo and get to the office. "Dammit. I gotta go." He gave Tanner's dick a kiss and cartwheeled out of bed.

Stunned, stuck with a raging hard-on that was about to explode, Tanner raised his head from the pillow and watched Skye dart to the bathroom like a bullet from a gun. Exhaling like he was exhausted, Tanner's head dropped back to the pillow and then he groaned loudly. "Aw, shit. One more second and that beautiful mouth of yours would have been full."

Skye quickly poked his head out the doorway and asked, "Do you mind if I use your shower, Tan?"

Gasping and horny as hell, Tanner answered, "Of course not. I'll get you a towel." He held his erect dick against his six-pack, so the bobbing of its extension didn't knock over lamps and shit when he took off for the linen closet.

In less than five minutes, Skye was finished showering and upstairs getting dressed. He winced when he put on another crispy shirt that felt like sand paper. The cleaner's had added too much starch to it even though he asked the bitch not to.

Meeting Tanner in the kitchen, Skye begged, "Can you save that boner for later?"

"Absolutely!" Tanner laughed as Skye eyed it greedily. He wished Skye's mouth was wrapped around his dick, sucking until a hot load pelted the back of his throat and painted his gorgeous face.

Skye mentioned to Tanner that he had a new client arriving first thing and if he showed up late, Jack would murder him on the spot.

If Skye had his way, he'd have stayed in bed and finished Tanner off, maybe taken his cock for another joy ride or traded places and let Tanner straddle the saddle. For now, that fantasy would definitely be a favored activity on the to-do list for later.

While Skye made sure he had everything packed in his attaché case, Tanner stood with his backside against the island countertop. He only had shorts on, looking appetizing as lean meat to Skye, ready to eat. His concrete six-pack and bulky chest seemed to fuck Skye's head up every time he saw them. He couldn't keep a level thought going if he tried, not with Tanner standing there like that. Lucky for Skye, that delectable cut of beefsteak was his to devour; anytime he wanted. Oddly enough, he had the fire that took his home out to thank for that.

Tanner regretfully reminded Skye that he had to be back at the station by four that afternoon, and like all the other times, wouldn't be home until the next day. Always an overnighter, sometimes a two-nighter.

Disappointed that there was going to be no one to come home to, Skye asked Tanner if he'd like to meet up for lunch. His appointment should be finished by late morning, so getting together sometime around one o'clock would work for Skye.

Tanner didn't think twice about it, quickly answering. "Sure. Name the place."

"Great. I'll call or text you." Skye looked at his watch out of habit. "All right, time to fly." He walked to the front door and opened it.

Following Skye, Tanner said, "Got everything you need?"

"If I had you, then yes." Skye smiled.

"Hey, wait a second. Aren't you forgetting something?" Tanner stepped face to face with Skye in the doorway and leaned in for a kiss.

Skye looked tensely across the street, stepped back inside, and kissed Tanner. "I'll have to get used to that." He pressed a hand to Tanner's chest and pushed off it and out the door.

Tanner wasn't sure what Skye was referring to just then; remembering to kiss him before leaving every day, or sneaking a kiss in public. Whichever it was, Tanner was willing to adjust, and hopefully Skye would too.

Chapter 18

Jack was waiting at the door to the office, looking for Skye to show up before the new clients for the Upper Northside mid-rise project arrived. Jack worried more than Skye did, especially when it came to business that entailed huge amounts of money and the potential for future projects. Jack wasn't a greedy man, just someone who wanted his greatest accomplishment to show he'd made an impact as an entrepreneur. He'd soon be able to relax and settle down, but not until Skye was standing in the office next to him.

Even with the Chicago traffic practically plugging up every street, Skye was on time. He was always punctual, so he never understood why Jack hounded him to be on time. If the meeting was at nine, Jack told him to be there at seven. That was his way to force punctuality.

They'd organized their plan of attack the day before. It included the exposition room set and ready to greet the guests. The first impression was ninety percent of the sale, so making their guests wait was not an option.

To start things off, Jack would be the main character in the production and Skye would be the supporting actor. It almost always worked that way, Jack started the show, and Skye finished it. After the deal was signed, as hopefully this one would be, Skye would steal the show and walk everybody to the grand opening where the ribbon would be snipped.

Getting started was always a bitch, and it was a good thing Jack had a handle on most of the meeting. As it turned out, Skye wasn't totally focused on the discussion. For the first time in the course of his career he had other things, like a certain stud, monopolizing his thoughts. Skye heard what he needed to hear, said what he had to say, and left the rest up to Jack.

During Skye's down time, which was when Jack had total control of the presentation, he turned his mind to Tanner, to how great his arms felt around him. For Skye, one of the better parts of being in Tanner's arms was when he shoved his fire hose of a dick up his tight white ass until it made him quake and shoot a load. If it weren't for the scheduled meeting, Skye would have had a mouth full of Tanner spunk before he left the bed.

Damn that meeting to hell.

On the upside, the meeting with the developers ended just after eleven-thirty. Thankfully they had to rush away without an in town lunch with Jack and Skye. That worked perfectly for Skye, not so much for Jack because that meant he was eating alone.

The clock was ticking closer to one o'clock and as agreed, Skye was on his way to the lunch date he'd made with his could-be-new-beau, Tanner. Damn he wanted that man as his boyfriend, but didn't want to rush such a hot guy into being tethered to him too soon. Skye knew he was crushing on Tanner because whenever the guy was in his head he got those annoying butterflies in his stomach.

While driving alone in his car, Skye thought about the morning's meeting and how well it went. He had a good feeling the agency had it in the bag. Those thoughts were short-lived, because his attention was once again taken over by images of Tanner: the man he was anxious to see at the café they'd decided on.

The timing was perfect. As soon as Skye parked his car and started walking to the door of the café, Tanner pulled in and saluted him, making his arrival known.

Skye continued walking to the entrance and waited there for Tanner, honestly pining to kiss him, but not able to do so in broad daylight. As he waited, Skye watched Tanner jog across the lot toward him with a smile on his face and his short hair trying to snap with the wind. He was wearing his firefighter blues that Skye liked so well. After seeing him completely naked the night before and clothed in uniform just then, he couldn't decide which way he liked him better. The man was hotter than friction during a hurried ass fucking any way he looked at him, so he picked his tongue up off the sidewalk and agreed on a tie score.

As soon as Tanner reached Skye, he crashed into him and hugged him, almost knocking him flat. Even though Skye felt tense to him, Tanner still hugged him. "Jeez I missed you."

Skye anxiously interrupted the hug, admitting, "Missed you too. How about we get our table before they give it away?" He didn't want to, but he pushed Tanner away with a couple of pats to his love handles. Manly pats, like those that friends might exchange.

Tanner was a little bothered by Skye's complete lack of affection toward him, but he understood and went with it. Maybe growth would come with time. Not all people are public huggers and kissers; maybe Skye was one of those people. Tanner didn't know for sure, but he could certainly feel the difference between their moments behind closed doors and those times when they stood under the sun or moon. But if that was the way Skye wanted it, then that was the way it would be.

When they reached the patio table outside the restaurant, Tanner fought the urge to pull back Skye's chair to help him sit first. He was a gentleman, and it was burning him up inside to know Skye wouldn't let him do something special for him. He'd not let him hold his hand, or give him a simple hug when the moment called for one. Tanner would work through it, he wanted to because he liked Skye. A lot.

They finished lunch in record time and as soon as the check was dropped, Skye quarreled with Tanner about who would cover the bill. Skye stood his ground and won.

Holding the restaurant door open for Skye, Tanner said, "I enjoyed that."

Skye stepped outside and answered. "It was good. We should come again soon."

"That's a plan, but I pay next time," Tanner argued.

"That's fair."

"Well, this is it. We part." Tanner stopped walking.

"Are you headed to the station from here or are you going home first?"

"To the station. I'll get there early, but that's fine."

"I'll be at the house early and then see you tomorrow night." Skye stepped to the side of his car.

Tanner followed him and said, "Skye. You can call my house home. I'd like it if you would."

"I'd like that." Skye smiled and then gripped the door handle.

Troubled, Tanner reached for Skye's arm and turned him back around. Their eyes met, Tanner's were a little misty because he liked Skye so much and his heart was hurting because Skye decided to walk away without as much as a brotherly hug.

Skye looked around the parking lot and then back at Tanner, not saying anything.

Tanner took Skye's hand as if his plan was to shake it, but instead covered it with his other putting Skye's in the middle. He looked at Skye, directly in his eyes and said, "Shit, Skye. I like you. A whole lot. I want to kiss you so badly right now that I feel daggers cutting my heart knowing you're holding back. We're not going to see each other until tomorrow, so can I at least get a hug from you?"

Skye had the same urges Tanner had. He wanted those kisses, even that hug, but struggled with public affection, always had.

"I really like you too, Tanner, maybe even more than that, but I... I'm just a miserable piece of shit when it comes to being comfortable enough to be openly affectionate with you or anybody in public. I stand a chance of losing everything because somebody else thinks that falling in love with another man is a bad thing. Many have lost their jobs for being gay. Some people don't even consider us valuable enough to live. I'm not ready to risk that."

"Skye. Hun. You won't lose your job. I can just about promise you that. Companies aren't able to get away with that anymore without huge risks." Tanner let go of Skye's hand, letting him find his comfort zone.

Skye took a minute to digest what Tanner just said and responded. "Everything is coming at me way too fast. I need a little time to adjust."

Tanner smiled and certainly agreed. "Of course. I don't want you to be forced into doing anything you don't want to do. But you should know that I couldn't go a single day without getting so much as a hug from you."

Checking the area first, Skye quickly gave Tanner a one armed hug that lasted less than two seconds and then stepped back just as quickly.

Shocked because he wasn't expecting it, Tanner said, "A good start, and that's all I need."

Skye opened up his car door and dropped behind the wheel. "It'll get better, I promise."

Tanner grinned and then saluted.

Chapter 19

"There he is. Yo, Tan. In here," Emmitt hollered, sitting in the great room on the sofa next to the window.

Tanner was already headed toward Emmitt, fist bumping the rest of the guys as he passed by them. If macho had a signature motion, bumping fists with other men would be it. No hugging, no kissing, no true emotion, just simple knuckle-to-knuckle contact that meant they were friends and nothing more.

After the shift transfer took place, the evening at the station turned out to be quiet. When it happened that they had no calls and a lot of free time, nobody knew what to do with themselves, other than get in each other's way. The guys scattered around the house like scavengers; milling for food, some hung out in the kitchen, a few in the garage, others wherever they wound up.

Tanner and Emmitt stayed in the great room on that same sofa by the window, not doing much of anything, merely lounging and chatting some. The boring crap firefighters usually do between drills and rescue missions.

While Emmitt played solitaire on his tablet, Tanner flipped through the pages of *USA Today,* mostly daydreaming while flicking the edge of the page he was looking at instead of reading it. Reality was rising, taking him on a different path than what he expected it to a few days ago. Everything he saw and read made him think of Skye.

Tanner turned another page and the next article he came across declared another American state had approved the legalization of gay marriage. The editorial was well written and mentioned that two men tied the knot in Key West, Florida. There was a photo showing them kissing on the beach, surrounded with family and friends. Once again, Tanner's thoughts went back to Skye, and he imagined the story was about the two of them. But by the way Skye reacted at the pool when Tanner kissed him, again when they were standing in the doorway at his house, and again at the restaurant, Tanner figured marriage was completely out of the question. At least it wasn't happening any time soon. Affection in public hit a nerve with Skye. Just thinking about it made Tanner's finger go crazy again, flicking back and forth at the edge of the page in a nervous tick. Planning to read the entire story later, he creased the page's corner before turning to the next.

Watching Tanner, Emmitt could tell there was a change in his mood from what it was a few days ago. He had a good idea the mood swing had something to do with a guy. "What does captain attractive have to be so depressed about? It's not like you, and it's kind of driving me nuts," Emmitt said.

Folding one corner of the paper down, Tanner stared at a spot over Emmitt's shoulder. His eyes were slits and looking heavy. It *was* late in the evening but that had nothing to do with how tired Tanner's eyes appeared. It was exhausting falling head over heels for Skye while trying to figure out if he really felt the same way. Tanner felt his emotions riding the proverbial roller coaster, going up, down, all over the place, and all he could do was wait for the ride to end. He wanted Skye to understand it was okay for two men to walk side by side down the street and even hold hands if they wanted to, but wasn't sure how to get that message through to him.

Getting nothing from Tanner after waiting patiently for a few minutes, Emmitt tried again. "So bro, what's going on with you? What's with the long face?"

Tanner heard him that time, snapped out of his daze, and said, "Sorry Emm, my head was in a cloud, thinking about someone I recently met."

Emmitt knew exactly who Tanner was talking about. "Is it that good-looking guy who came here to see you the other day?" he asked.

Tanner's answer was short, "Yep... him."

"Why aren't you happier?"

"I am... sort of. It's just that he puts so much space between us when we're in public together. I'm not used to that."

"You just met him, Tan. Give the guy time to adjust. Maybe he's old school and wants to make sure he likes you first," Emmitt said.

"I don't think that's what it is. He's fine when it's just the two of us. I already found that out." Tanner put the paper down on the table where he'd gotten it from.

"What's that mean? Did you bang him?"

Tanner gave Emmitt the stink eye and then said, "Actually I did. He's so fucking hot, I couldn't wait, and neither could he."

"That was quick. You got his name first didn't you?" Emmitt grinned.

"Don't be an ass. His name is Skye, and he's staying at my house because he doesn't have any place to go right now. The night started pleasantly enough by the pool, one thing led to another and we ended up in my bed fucking our brains out. The sex was super-hot and the emotional connection I felt with him was like nothing I've ever experienced. With anyone. Everything seemed to fit so perfectly. I think he could be my real deal."

"Whoa… Whoa, bud. You can hold back on the rump-ranger rendezvous details." Emmitt raised a hand, putting a stop to Tanner's elaborate explanation. "So he moved in, huh? I hope he isn't crazy and everything is still in its place when you get home."

"I'm a good judge of character, so I'm pretty sure he's not a thief." Tanner was about to tell Emmitt how much he liked Skye, wanted to date him and keep fucking him exclusively. He was interrupted by the fire-bell and an announcement that a building on Broadway North was burning.

That familiar rush of adrenaline raced through the entire team as soon as the alarm went off and the place turned into organized chaos until the trucks pulled out into the street.

Sitting in the cab together on the way to the fire, Emmitt snapped his fingers in front of Tanner and said, "Hey, bud, you with us?"

"Yeah-yeah." Tanner nodded, his mind still on Skye.

By the time they got to the fire location, flames had already taken over most of the building, flashes snapped from every window and black smoke billowed into the sky above it.

Emmitt headed for the upper floor, motioning for Tanner to follow. At the top of the stairs were two doors. Standing next to them, Emmitt said, "You go left, I'll take the right. Call out if you need any help in there and I'll do the same."

Tanner went through the open door, urgently searching for anybody inside.

While Tanner was heroically fighting fires in the night, Skye was at home, randomly scrolling through all the channels on the television because he couldn't sleep. Out of six hundred channels, he couldn't seem to find anything that held his attention or that he hadn't already seen. He stopped flipping when he found the local news. It was eleven-thirty at night, so it seemed an obvious choice. He heard the meteorologist mention there'd be a fifty percent chance of rain, which meant it may or may not rain, and then took a wild guess that the expected temperature would be somewhere in the seventies.

Skye dropped down on the sofa, throwing his feet onto the ottoman in front of him. He started to relax a little, getting comfortable, when the news anchor mentioned "Breaking News." Over his shoulder was a video monitor displaying a building burning on Broadway North.

Skye quickly sat up and froze. Just then the news station went to a commercial break. *What horrible timing!*

During the badly timed disruption, Skye ran to the kitchen where he'd left his phone. He tapped Tanner's face to dial, but hung up before it reached the last number. Instead, he waited for the broadcast to return with more details on the fire. He tried to calm down; telling himself there was no need to get hysterical. Not yet. Tanner fought fires like the one on the news almost every day, was trained for it, and he may not even be at that particular location.

The two minutes that Skye waited for the news to come back on seemed like ten. He dreaded the unknown, hated it. That wasn't helping his nerves, which were already pricking every part of his being.

"Thank God. Finally," Skye mumbled, while standing in front of the television screen, looking at the building on fire, trying to get a glimpse of Tanner someplace at the scene. Skye knew it was Tanner's team, he recognized the placards on the trucks, even a few of the men he met at the station the other day. He held a hand worriedly over his mouth while watching for the cameras to pan and show him Tanner.

The reporter on the scene mentioned the possibility of fatalities, exaggerating his words in a way that made the situation seem more severe than it probably was. The reporter kept using words like massive explosions, intense heat, deadly flames, and other phrases to grab the attention of the viewer. *How could they?*

Flipping out because he never saw Tanner on the news, Skye went for his phone again, tapping Tanner's face to dial his number. He let the call go through this time, and it rang a few times with no answer, but he hung up when the voicemail message system kicked on.

Skye didn't know all the firefighters' rules yet, so he wasn't sure they carried personal communication devices with them when battling flames. But something told him Tanner didn't have his cell phone with him.

Skye and Tanner were emotionally linked and that strong connection had Skye feeling like Tanner was in trouble. He couldn't seem to get the idea out of his head. Skye wasn't ready to lose him. Not yet. To set his mind at ease, Skye needed to know for sure that Tanner was okay. Sticking around home wasn't going to give him the answers he was looking for.

Nervous and feeling the heat in his face rising, Skye put on a shirt and ran to the car. He quickly jammed the shifter into drive and rolled into the street without looking.

As he sped down the boulevard on his way to the fire station, headlamps from oncoming cars pierced his eyes. He called Tanner's cell again and pleaded. "Answer, Tanner. Please answer the phone?"

An unfamiliar mechanical voice picked up. The one that always lets the caller know the person they are trying to reach is unavailable. "Damn! Shit!" Skye cussed, shaking the phone as if that was going to help fix it and then hit the call button again.

Skye ended the call when he heard the same voice as before. "Dammit!" He tossed the phone to the passenger seat and it bounced onto the floor. That time he said, "Fuck."

It took Skye almost twenty minutes to get to the station, and by the time he got there, his heart rate was elevated way above normal. He left the car without shutting the door and took off through the garage to find Tanner, or anyone else inside who could tell him where Tanner was.

Sitting at the kitchen table were two firefighters, both without smiles. They looked like something was wrong. Skye felt in his gut that the muted looks on their faces had something to do with Tanner. He stood staring until one of the guys asked how they could help him. Skye took a few steps closer and asked, "Is Tanner available?" His voice came out shaky.

"How do you know Tanner?" the lieutenant asked. The name embroidered on his shirt was Aaron.

Skye hesitated, not certain how to explain who he was to Tanner. Instead of telling them he was a one-night stand, he said he was his housemate and was concerned about him because he hadn't come home or answered any of his calls. Everything he said was the truth.

The guys knew who Skye was, remembered him from the other day.

Aaron pulled out a chair at the table for Skye and asked him to sit. Trying to stay positive, Aaron put on a fake smile and tried to figure a gentle way of telling Skye there was an accident during a rescue and Tanner was involved.

Skye tried to hide his face but it was obvious to everybody at the table he was turning white. He had good reason to look the way he did. None of the guys were smiling or joking around the way they were the last time he was there. He knew something very bad had happened and could sense it was Tanner. There was an empty feeling shifting inside him, like the connection he had with Tanner was breaking.

Aaron held back a minute before telling Skye the news about Tanner heroically pulling someone from the second floor of a burning building. On his way out with the victim, the floor under their feet collapsed and they both went down. He told him that Tanner was taken to the nearest hospital by ambulance and they were waiting for further news regarding his condition.

Skye looked stunned; his face turned whiter than it was before. He was so scared, he felt like a ghost had passed right through him. Stuttering, he asked, "Can... Um... Can... or are we able to go see him? Where is he?"

Still trying to hold his smile, Aaron told Skye the name of the hospital where Tanner was taken.

Skye knew of it. It was the same one they took him to when he needed to be cared for the other day. When he nervously stood up to thank

Aaron, Skye unintentionally knocked the chair he was sitting in to the floor. He spun to pick it up, but Aaron grabbed hold of his arm and told him not to worry about it.

Skye turned, shaking his head. "I've gotta get going."

Noticing how upset Skye was, Aaron said, "Hang on, Skye. I'll take you there."

"I'm all right. I know where the hospital is." Skye accidentally dropped the keys to the floor.

Aaron let go of Skye and said, "You're not all right. I'm taking you."

"But I'll need my car to bring Tanner home," Skye said optimistically.

"I'll drive it." Aaron picked up the keys. "Let's get going."

Chapter 20

Love doesn't stop when two people are in different places. Miles apart or right next door.

Aaron drove to the hospital while Skye rode along with him. It was clearly the better idea, considering Skye wasn't handling the situation well.

Unable to stand being separated from Tanner any longer, Skye pushed Aaron to go faster. Skye had to be by Tanner's side, needed to know what was going on with him. If he didn't get to Tanner soon, he would surely burst; especially now, when Tanner probably needed him most.

On the way, Skye's eyes misted over, he was on the verge of crying. He really liked Tanner and was terrified of what he was going to hear or find when he got to the hospital. He felt a great connection with Tanner that he knew was real, solid, and honest; one that was stronger than anything he'd ever felt or even expected before. Skye was part of Tanner's life now and deep down he wanted to love that man, or truthfully; could easily love that man.

Displaying affection was never part of who Skye was. He rarely showed it or gave it. Even when growing up, Skye was never exposed to physical love, he'd not been around it, in public or in places that were private. It just wasn't part of his life and somehow that wall stayed with him well into adulthood.

The tear Skye was holding back finally rolled down his cheek as he realized he could lose Tanner. Another one followed when he thought about the way he'd left Tanner at the restaurant earlier in the day. He hated himself for not giving Tanner the hug he wanted, despised himself for being too scared to show him how he felt. Skye would give anything to go back to that restaurant and start again, display how much he liked Tanner, and show it to him in public.

They finally reached the hospital and after circling the outside parking lot, Aaron eventually found a place to park on the forth level of the hospital's parking structure. Wasting no time, they hurried down the stairs instead of waiting for the elevator to come get them.

Finding the guest registration and checking in, Skye speed-walked through the hallway ahead of Aaron to the room they were told Tanner was in. Before Skye reached the door to Tanner's room, he saw several of the station's brothers standing nearby, dressed in uniform, holding coffee cups and what looked like bagels. He recognized Emmitt leaning against the wall staring at the lights in the ceiling. The image Skye saw didn't look good.

Skye slowed his pace to a crawl and then stopped, not wanting to see what was up ahead. Aaron caught up and stood there with him, so close they appeared to be lovers. Whatever Skye was about to see could completely break his heart. His chin quivered while the corners of his mouth tugged downward, forcing sadness to his face. He blinked the tears back before taking another step.

A few of the waiting firefighters glanced in Aaron and Skye's direction at the same time. Then Emmitt looked their way, and lifted himself off the wall before turning toward them.

When Skye met up with Emmitt, he stared silently and waited for any details he had on Tanner. Good or bad, he needed to hear it.

A smile crossed Emmitt's mouth and he said, "Tanner will be glad you're here. He's been asking for you since the EMTs brought him in."

Skye started to smile, but still looked gloomy. "What happened?"

"He was being himself: a hero, and fell through the floor with a kid in his arms. Luck followed him down because when he hit the first floor, a mattress was waiting. The guys have been teasing him about his ability to bounce, so make sure you bring that up when you see him."

Skye felt the weight dropping from his shoulders when he heard that Tanner was going to be okay. He purred, "Thank God."

Emmitt quickly peeked in on Tanner and reported back to Skye. "He has a few bruises and a swollen ankle, but he'll be fine. They gave him some painkillers to get him by, so he's a bit lazy with his speech. Don't let that freak you out; it's only because of the drugs they're dumping into him."

Skye dipped his head around Emmitt's shoulder to have a look at Tanner, then asked, "Can I go in right now?"

Squeezing Skye's shoulder, Emmitt said, "Yes, of course. He'd like that."

Skye stepped around Emmitt and started to walk through the doorway, but before he made it too far, Emmitt added, "Hey Skye, I'm glad... I mean, *we're* glad you came. Tanner has mumbled your name a few times, asking about you. And Skye... everybody at the station is happy about Tanner meeting somebody he really seems to like."

Skye gave Emmitt a grateful grin and then went inside to see Tanner. He huddled up close to Tanner's bedside and combed his fingers softly through his grimy hair.

Feeling a gentle touch grace his brow, Tanner rolled his head across the pillow and looked at Skye with heavy lids. He spoke in a slow relaxed drawl. "Hi. Glad you came. But please don't look at me because I'm hideous."

Skye smiled behind his tears, keeping his frightened emotions hidden. "You're not hideous, Tanner, and I'm happy to know you're alright. I couldn't muster an educated thought until I saw you."

Tanner whispered, "You're sweet and I love you for that."

Skye's hand moved from Tanner's head to his shoulder. "By the looks of things, you're not going anywhere for a while are you?" Skye asked.

Just then, Emmitt stepped into the room and

answered for Tanner. "He has a slight concussion, so they want to keep an eye on him until morning. They'll let him go tomorrow."

"I'm fine with that. It's best to be safe." Sky backed away from Tanner and asked Emmitt, "Do you think they'll have a problem if I stay in the room with him for a while?"

Emmitt answered, "Don't worry about that. They know all of us here and we're regularly given exceptions to the visitor rules. I'll clear it with the admin desk."

Skye thanked Emmitt; taking a minute to adjust to how pleasant he and everybody from the station seemed to be. Skye wasn't used to that, and it made him think an open relationship with Tanner could work; or at least it would around those guys.

Before the brotherhood left the hospital, each of them made sure Tanner knew he was still part of the team. They teased and mocked him the same way they always did. With critical jibes and jeers, showing love in a manly way.

A few days ago, the hospital shoe was on the other foot, Skye in the bed with Tanner stretched out in the chair beside him.

Time passed, and the hospital turned quiet later in the night. Almost like there were no emergency issues during the early a.m. hours, or they locked the doors so nobody could get in.

Tanner had drifted off to sleep a while before, with Skye sitting in the chair watching over him, making sure he stayed comfortable. Not knowing if it was allowed or not, Skye moved furniture around the room so he could pull the chair tightly up against the side of Tanner's bed. While he sat next to him, Skye held Tanner's hand the same way Tanner did his when their roles were swapped. Their fingers locked together perfectly, the touch was warm, and their pulses actually synchronized. Skye drifted off to sleep, holding the hand of the man he was planning to love.

The nurse quietly crept into the room, waking Skye with a gentle shake. "Good morning, Skye. I need to ask you to wake up now. The doctor will be in shortly to do a final check on our friend," he whispered to him.

Skye blinked his eyes a few times, adjusting to the soft light coming in from the hallway. He stretched, pulled his hand free from Tanner's, and pushed the chair back where it belonged.

Tanner woke when he felt Skye pull his hand away. He was a bit bleary from the painkillers, but fully awake. His mouth felt dry when he said, "Good morning."

Shortly after Tanner woke, the doctor let him know he was free to go.

While they waited for the nurse to return with Tanner's walking papers and any follow-up instructions from the doctor, Skye gathered all of Tanner's belongings and helped him back into his station blues.

It took about forty more minutes before that happy moment came when the nurse said, "As soon as you sign here, here, and here, you're free to go."

Chapter 21

"This is nice," Tanner said.

"What is?" Skye asked.

"Me with my arm draped over your shoulder, leaning against you on the way to the car. I'm feeling loved." Tanner took one step at a time, literally, but he so badly wanted to kiss Skye.

"I couldn't let you hobble the halls alone, now could I?" Skye said.

As they rode the elevator to the fourth floor where the car was parked, Skye gripped Tanner's waist, locking his thumb over the belt behind his back to keep him from losing his balance and going down. No telling how long that lazy drug was going to be keeping his system hostage. Better to be safe than sorry. No one was hitting the dirt on Skye's watch.

The elevator stopped and the doors opened up to the garage where Skye parked the car and before they stumbled any further, Skye asked Tanner if he wanted to stay behind while Skye went to get the car. Tanner didn't like that idea at all, and latched on tighter to Skye's side as they hobbled to the car like conjoined twins.

Skye was rather surprised he remembered what level Aaron parked the car on during their harried rush to get to Tanner. He successfully located it with the help of the panic button on the key remote.

"Here's your carriage, my love." Skye opened the passenger door and lowered Tanner into the seat.

Before Tanner removed his arm from around Skye's neck, he whispered into his ear. "Thank you for being here with me, Skye." Then backed away and spoke a little louder. "I wouldn't have wanted anybody else to carry me home."

"Don't be silly. I wanted to be here. Because"—Skye stopped—"Well because...." He glanced away while he lifted Tanner's arm from around his neck and let it drop gently to his lap.

"Wait. Because what?" Tanner looked up at Skye.

"It's nothing. Let's get you home so you can rest." Sky ran around to the driver's door, climbed in, and started the car; pushed the shifter into drive and headed home.

While staring out the front windshield, Tanner asked, "Did you call your office to let them know you were with me today? You are staying with me aren't you?" Tanner sounded a little like he was begging.

"Done," Skye said. "I told Jack I needed to take a personal day. Knowing I was practically burnt to a crisp, he understood without question."

"Great. It'll be nice having you around." Tanner took a chance by placing his hand over Skye's and left it there, hoping he wouldn't pull away.

Skye didn't budge. He left his hand on the console shifter the whole way home, capped by Tanner's and made sure he knew; "If a nurse is what you need, I'm your man."

When they arrived at the house, Tanner made a beeline to the sofa and dropped down into it. Skye followed, sitting next to him, so close he was almost in Tanner's lap. Skye kissed him, holding the kiss so long that their breathing was labored through nostrils alone, cool air in, hot air out. About a minute passed before their passion simmered to a slow burn, taking them from hot and heavy to cool and light.

Holding the kiss even longer, Tanner whispered into Skye's mouth. "I don't want you to ever leave, Skye. I like the idea of coming home to you, knowing you're here."

Skye replied as best he could while submitting to Tanner's warm mouth over his own. "I look forward to every homecoming."

Thrilled and taking Skye's answer as confirmation he was sticking around, Tanner swept the warmth of his lips across Skye's, trailed feathery kisses along his jawline and stopped below his ear, hot breath shattering Skye's senses as Tanner suckled his lobe.

Suffering through Tanner's passionate torture, Skye trembled. The musky scent of burnt timber from Tanner's hair added a desire within Skye to open himself up and take him deep. The urge to make love to Tanner was strong, so much so that Skye wanted to strip bare and ride Tanner's stone hard cock right there in the living room. Instead, he changed places with Tanner, giving back the same mind blowing foreplay so thoughtfully granted him.

Even though still a bit drowsy on drugs, an orgasm mounted quickly within Tanner. His chest rapidly rose and fell with every gasp for air. He tried to hold back his release but couldn't, his body went tight, jerked forward and he came in his pants. He groaned as semen spit from his cock, soaking the front of his blues, spreading rapidly across his hip and down his thigh in a way that looked like a hose was leaking.

The pungent scent of Tanner's semen overpowered the air between them, arousing a man like Skye, making his cock throb with a dire need to blast Tanner with what was churning inside of him. He wanted to fist himself to a full release, but instead fibbed. "I didn't mean for that to happen. Not yet anyway."

Body twitching, Tanner huffed. "Fuck that apology." He gasped. "That was awesome." He shuddered and jerked still. "You made me cum with kisses alone. That's fucking talent." He panted. "I fucking need to keep you, Skye. Forever."

Skye's own cock was stone hard and didn't seem like it was ready to settle down. He tried to ignore it and queried, "Right then, what's in it for me?"

Tanner withdrew, unable to contain his grin. "All this, my lovely" — he dragged the back of his nails down the front of his chest—"and a place beside me in my bed, starting with tonight if you would."

"Since you put it that way, I'd be happy to keep you company." Skye hugged Tanner, held him for a while, massaging the nape of his neck.

Tanner gave Skye a tight squeeze and said, "That'll be great, but keeping me company isn't really what I had in mind. I want you around for more than that."

Skye loosened his hold on Tanner and asked, "You mean like a housekeeper?"

"You're not being serious, are you?" Tanner replied.

Skye laughed. That's it, just laughed.

Tanner let go of Skye, leaned back against the sofa, and took hold of his hand. "I like you Skye. A whole lot. I know the time we've known each other has been super short, but I like you more than I've ever liked anyone before. It's crazy, I know, but I can't stop thinking about you, Skye. Look what you've just done to me! Neither of us touched my dick. I came in my pants from simply touching you, being near you. That is a huge connection that's probably meant to be. Shit, I'm rambling, but I have you on my mind every minute of the day: nonstop, actually. This may seem perverted, but I've even dreamt about you and woke up with one of the hardest erections I think I'd ever had in my life, I swear." Tanner admitted all of this at once. All the things Skye felt, too.

Skye blushed because he'd never heard anybody talk to him the way Tanner did. Skye squeezed Tanner's hands in a way that told him he'd never let go.

Whispering, Tanner asked, "Will you stay?"

Skye couldn't stand it. On an impulse, he lunged for Tanner, kissing him hard, locking their mouths together, his securely over Tanner's. Then there was tongue, forceful and punishing.

Tanner breathed into Skye's mouth. "Hot damn, Skye. Is that a yes?"

Gasping, Skye pulled air from Tanner's lungs and hummed, "Mmm-hmm."

"Shit, you've got me rock hard again. Already. I'd be lying if I told you I'll be able to wait 'til the lights go down to shower you with my cum or fuck you again." Tanner was almost hissing, his desire was robbing him of breath.

Skye smirked and said, "But you're kind of damaged. How are you going to bang my tight ass without aggravating your bones and bruises?"

"Trust me, I'll manage. A hot fuck and a gushing orgasm trumps pain any day. I just proved that to you. I've had many injuries before, and compared to them; these dents and dings are nothing," Tanner assured Skye. "To ease my bones and bruises, as you call them, we could trade places this time. You take the top and I'll just lay there on the bottom and let you have at me. What do you say?"

"What? Are you nuts? I don't want you lying there like a dead fish. That would be fucked up. I need you there with me or at least acting like you're enjoying what I'm doing to you."

"All right, I'll wiggle some. Will that work?" Tanner laughed.

"Uh… Let me think… Nope, still fucked up."

"So it's a no?"

"I didn't say that."

"Then it's a yes?"

"Decide on a safe word and I'll think about giving you the big one." Skye grinned sinisterly, he really wanted to power-drive Tanner's ass, but preferred not to give his body any more discomfort than what he already had.

Tanner's brow lifted. "My ankles are what's tender, not my ass. But if a safe word is what'll get you to my bed and into my ass, then I'll make one up."

"Settled. Get ready for the ride of your life."

"Oh, Gawd. There it is. Boner alert." Tanner glanced at his dick and saw it move, pressing upward against the already semen-soaked fabric of his pants.

Skye laid a hand over Tanner's erection and told him, "You need to put that thing away until a safe word comes to mind, one you'll remember and won't shock me to hear."

Tanner sort of agreed while watching his erection deflate. "I don't need a safe word, but if you insist, I'll come up with one. I honestly don't understand why a safe word would be something other than, ouch, halt, whoa or stop. Those seem to be the most logical choices, right?"

With regret, Skye slid his hand off Tanner's dick and mentioned; "I've wondered about that myself, but I'm sure there's a good reason. Next time you're at a bondage & discipline convention, be sure to ask."

Tanner reached out and took hold of Skye's hand, not letting him get too far and said, "When I have a chance I will, but right now, I'd like to help you ejaculate. I have a few choice targets I want you to aim for."

"Sweet thought, but…." Skye tugged.

"But what?" Tanner could easily pop off another load in less than five minutes, ready to stick his dick inside Skye and fuck his brains out, finish him off like he should have earlier.

Skye cupped his hands to the sides of Tanner's beautiful face, below his ears with fingers stroking his dark blond hair, then told him the truth. "How about you shower first. The smoky smudges make you appear more damaged than you probably are and you smell like a chimney sweep. I'd be happy to help you to your bed chamber if you'd like."

Tanner quickly realized the one drawback about that plan. Hot sex with Skye would have to wait a little longer.

Chapter 22

When Tanner reappeared from his shower, he was surrounded by the scent of an ocean breeze. It was much more pleasant than the smoke bomb he smelled of before he went in. His scratches and bruises stood out more fiercely against his clean skin.

Skye was in the kitchen preparing an early afternoon breakfast. He looked up when he smelled Tanner in the room and said, "Wow-wee, you gleam when you clean up, almost as bright as the sunshine."

"It smells so good in here, like a top-notch diner." Tanner stood beside Skye, wrapped an arm around his waist, and kissed his temple.

"Okay, dearest; it's ready. Take the juice glasses to the table and have a seat." Skye followed Tanner with a plate in each hand and sat across the table from him.

"Good job with breakfast. Where did you get all this?" Tanner asked.

"You had everything I needed in your pantry. Didn't you know it was there? Don't you cook?"

"Had no clue, and do I look like I cook?"

"You look like a man who can do anything he sets his mind to. But that's fine; I'll take on that role from now on."

"Did you make sure the ingredients hadn't expired?" Tanner stopped, fork midway to his mouth.

"I did." Skye grinned at Tanner's worried expression.

"Are you a chef too?"

"In a matter of speaking, I've become one. If I hadn't, I'd go hungry."

"You did well with what little I had in that closet."

"I can manage even if there's very little to work with." Skye smirked.

Tanner finished his breakfast quickly because he was starving, probably due to the fact he hadn't eaten anything since their lunch the day before. An I.V. and morphine didn't constitute real food, nor did it fill an empty stomach. He pushed his plate forward, topped both their mugs with fresh hot coffee, then leaned back in his chair and stared at Skye.

"What are you gawking at?" Skye looked at Tanner over the rim of his mug.

"I'd like to ask you something, Skye."

"Go ahead, shoot."

Tanner hesitated before telling Skye what was on his mind. He hadn't told Skye about his upcoming commencement from cadet to a full-fledged firefighter yet. He hadn't been sure Skye would want to go to the ceremony if he had asked him to be his guest. He planned on mentioning it to him several times, but whenever it came to mind, Skye wasn't around or the timing didn't seem right. As Tanner got to know Skye better over the past few days, coming to feel closer to him, the more he wanted him with him at his graduation.

Skye asked again, "What did you want to ask me?"

Tanner touched Skye on the arm and said, "I know its last minute, but this evening I'll be awarded my firefighter's shield and I'd like you to be there when I'm honored with it. Would you be my date? It starts at seven."

Skye was taken aback, unprepared for an invitation to such an important life event, one where he would be another man's companion.

"Wow. I'm honored. Is it formal? What'll I wear? Will there be many guests?" Driven by panic, the questions just fell out of Skye's mouth.

Tanner was well aware that Skye was good at hiding his true feelings behind a public front, so was pleasantly surprised by his seemingly positive animated response. Tanner tried to help him remain calm by keeping his words soft spoken. "All the guys from the station will be there along with a few guests and their companions. Not a large group, but not a small gathering either," he told Skye truthfully.

"You said tonight, right?" Sky nervously picked up the dirty plates and carried them to the sink where he rinsed them under hot water before putting them in the dishwasher. Not paying attention to what he was doing, his mind focused more on being in public with a male date, and people finding out he was gay; he burned his hand while moving a plate through the steaming downpour. "Shit!" He dropped it and reflexively shouted.

Tanner left his seat to help Skye, or save him from burning himself further. He was wondering what'd really caused the expletive to fly, unbidden from his mouth. Was it because Skye burned his hand, or because he was distraught about being seen in public as another man's date? Tanner knew how much Skye liked him, could feel it, but also knew how difficult it was for Skye to express his true feelings for another man in a public setting.

"Let me help you with that," Tanner said.

"I'm okay. It's just another burn," Skye said.

Tanner turned the water to a colder setting and placed Skye's hand under the stream. "Keep it under the water flow for a few minutes, you'll be fine."

"Damn, your water's hot," Skye mentioned. "Thanks for the speedy rescue, even though I would've survived this one on my own."

"Don't mention it. Heat is my specialty."

"Should I put butter on it?"

"Gawd no, that seals the heat in."

"Shit. I've been doing that my entire life. I always thought it helped."

"Very common misconception, it's best to cool it down under cold water. Just keep your hand in the water while I finish cleaning up." Tanner loaded the dishwasher and put everything away.

By the time Tanner was finished, Skye was

fanning the air over his hand with the uninjured hand. "Thanks for the tip about butter versus water."

"Consider it your tip of the day, and think of it like this; if butter were the better option for bringing down the flames, we'd be spraying lard from our hoses instead of water."

"Clever man. Hence the reason you're getting a metal tonight." Sky winked.

There was an unspoken current of thoughts passed between them, including some unsteady ones from Skye's direction. It wasn't all that difficult for Tanner to see, since Skye's raised-shoulders-no-neck tension spoke louder than any words he could have confessed.

Tanner wasn't going to beg Skye to go with him to the ceremony, but instead looked at him with eyes that reflected the hope of his heart. Puppy dog eyes had worked for him many times before, so he used them, hoping those weepy greens would work in his favor that time.

"Oh, Gawd, don't look at me like that," Skye groaned. The rumble of the dishwasher next to him matched his tone, but felt more like a drill to his skull. The continuous rotation of the motor was rattling his nerves, which felt like they were being torn from his flesh with crippling force.

Skye was aware of his issues with love and the affection that went hand in hand with it. Most of them stemmed from a young age. With the exception of his father, Tag, who had never shown any anguish toward Skye for being who he was meant to be, Skye had been told many times by others closest to him that he should be ashamed of who he was; that his choices were wrong. He knew when they used the word "choice," they were referring to his attraction toward men as if it were something he had control over. His fascination with and attraction to men had never been his decision. It was the way he was made, he'd been born that way, and there was no changing whom he was. Skye always ground his teeth when his family reminded him they considered his sexuality to be a choice.

He fought people on the meaning of that word a few times, explaining that a choice was deciding if you prefer chicken to fish, or fries over a salad. How a young man's dick reacted when he spotted a boy or a girl in the room just happened. People don't choose to be gay. Being gay is one of those God-given bonuses intended to broaden the world's perspective on love as well as make it a more whimsical place.

The harsh words Skye had grown up hearing had left him feeling empty and cold. Like he was in a concrete basement with no color, just lots of nothingness where everything was frozen over. Those words resulted in his feeling alone and untouchable. It was a cold dark place he'd never been at ease with and he no longer wanted to be stuck there.

Recalling it all, a feeling of despair washed over Skye. He fought it, but the figurative door to that dark, cold place was pulsating in his mind's eye. It was trying to break open and pull him back into the darkness; that's what scared him the most.

Tanner noticed the melancholy that had come over Skye, and didn't want him to feel pressured into doing something he wasn't comfortable with. He tried to lighten the mood. "You can stay here tonight. Do the laundry, clean the house if you'd like. The vacuum's in the coat closet next to the garage." Tanner's lame attempt at a joke got surprising results.

Skye's eyes brightened when Tanner said that, he understood his humor and what he was doing. He still tried to explain to Tanner why he was so cold when being observed by those from the outside. He hated being judged or ridiculed for being gay, absolutely despised how it made him feel. Always tried to keep his distance from it, and if anybody brought it up, he'd find a way to change the subject. He was never good at confrontation about his sexuality, but this time it was different for him. This time it was all about a man he was falling in love with and wanted to be with desperately. If he planned on being with Tanner in any real, long-lasting way, he was damned well going to force himself to change for the better. Tanner wasn't worth losing over somebody else's problem with his orientation. It wasn't his issue anymore, but theirs. Skye felt free, as open as his name, once he recognized that fact deep in his gut.

Chapter 23

The day passed by quickly and before they knew it, the clock struck four in the afternoon.

"Holy crap, did you see the time?" Skye squealed, and then chattered nervously. "We need to get you ready for your big moment. What are you wearing to an event like this? Did you set it aside?"

Tanner crumpled his brow. "Whoa there, stallion; you're working up a sweat. I've got it covered. I'll be wearing a formal jacket I've earned. It's the same type that all cadets wear when they become official firefighters," he explained calmly.

"Okay. You're right. Whew. Calm down, Skye, taaaake it easy." Skye's hands fell to his sides after patting the sweat from his brow.

Tanner chuckled at Skye's irrational behavior. The event was no big deal for Tanner, certainly nothing to get worked up over.

"I'm good now. Do I need to iron anything for you?" Skye offered.

"That's all taken care of and it's hanging at the station."

"The station? Is that where this ceremony is at?"

"We start there, but the formal part of the service is at a banquet hall across the street from the firehouse. Easy access."

"Well then, let's at least get you started with a T-shirt and a tie." Skye reached for Tanner's hand and walked him down the hall.

As soon as they entered the master bedroom, Skye lunged for Tanner, walking him backward toward the bed. He kissed him fiercely while struggling to open up the placket on his button down shorts. He needed Tanner's body to help him relax.

Tanner impatiently tugged on Skye's shirt, pushing it over his head, exposing his muscled chest and rugged shoulders; Tanner's favorite part of Skye, other than his face, his abs, ass, legs and thick dick.

With increasing desire to feel Tanner's bare chest against his own, Skye gave him a hand at shedding his shirt. He watched Tanner's strong stomach and chest flex as he lifted his arms above his head. Skye could only mutter the words he'd used before. "Holy fuck, you're fucking ripped." All that ladder climbing and carrying people out of burning buildings must have helped put Tanner in such great shape. He was fucking built like a steel dump truck and the mechanics of the steam-punk tattoo arching down his bicep made him appear harder.

Deeper fascination reigned over Skye the

second he laid his hands against Tanner's chest. His muscles, built by tough labor, drew Skye in as his most favored attractions. Moving slowly, he traced down his guttered abs until his impatient hands dived under the waistband and into the warm hair surrounding his growing dick.

Tanner trembled when Skye touched him and the swelling in his briefs vastly increased.

As Tanner's cock sprang to life, the feeling of it traveling densely across the back of his hand made Skye quiver with desire. He hungrily attacked Tanner's mouth, tongue bypassing teeth and demanding a deeper kiss.

Skye wanted to manhandle Tanner, give him the sendoff he deserved for earning that well-merited badge. Gripping his shoulders, Skye firmly pushed Tanner backward to the bed and climbed over top of him, balancing his weight on a single knee while one hand found a place on his chest. The recently trimmed hair growing back pricked his palm.

Lifting himself from Tanner's grasp, Skye stood to remove every bit of his own clothing. Standing completely nude, he overlooked the man lying on his back like an offering, whom he was going to bed and bang until he burst.

Tanner had seen Skye's dick size from previous encounters, but seeing it in its erect magnitude again took him by surprise. Astounded, he lay waiting for the intrusion of a lifetime, anticipating how far up inside him Skye would go. He felt his asshole twitch like it was getting started without them.

Smiling and focusing on romance, Skye

leaned into Tanner and tendered delicate kisses to his abdomen. His warm breath caused tremors through Tanner's tingling flesh. Tanner lay back wearing only his snug-fitting briefs, erection visibly stiff beneath the fine black fabric, looking incredibly enticing to Skye.

Moving in, Skye positioned his body over Tanner, holding his balance on the heels of both hands. He looked down on his submissive fireman, gazing at him, and breathing shallowly.

Enthused by the vision of Skye above him, Tanner's heart pounded and he sensed his back entrance flex and contract again, begging for that much-wanted grand invasion.

Skye lowered himself, pinning Tanner beneath his gym-hardened body. Infatuated, they lay kissing, mouth against mouth, and heart tapping heart. Maintaining a lip-locked connection, Skye slid his body to lie at Tanner's side. With an emotion-filled touch, he skimmed his fingernails down Tanner's rippled stomach until he reached the profound spot between his legs.

Tanner lost himself when he gripped Skye's erection, feeling it rapidly increase in size, getting thicker and standing stiff. Tanner held the shaft, struggling to meet finger and thumb, fisting Skye and stroking him slowly.

Leaning into Tanner's chest, Skye traced a wet tongue across his perked up nipples. The grace of his slippery tongue intensified Tanner's tremors, making him moan; wanting more. While nipping and licking his chest, Skye slid his hand back and forth along Tanner's shaft, stroking it slowly to maximize its size; then removing his briefs.

Skye continued with tiny kisses across Tanner's chest, increasing suction when he reached a nub, taking his time on each one. From there he dragged his wet lips and tongue over the hills and valleys that blocked Tanner's six-pack. His body quaked when Skye's lips capped and gently suckled the crown of his raging erection. The heat from his breath against his velvety gland flushed over him, forcing a fiery moan to escape Tanner, one that quickly turned gritty as Skye took him all the way in his mouth.

Pleasured quakes gripped Tanner for several minutes while Skye sucked and swallowed what he could of his pumped up erection. Feeling the pressure building inside himself, Tanner begged Skye to stop.

Backing off, Skye reluctantly slid Tanner from his mouth and repositioned himself atop him; kissing Tanner's cheeks, his nose, and then his lips. Face to face with Tanner, Skye ground their erections together, rhythmically rocking against him. Welcoming Skye, Tanner extended the invitation by securely locking his ankles behind Skye's back. The weight of Skye's body on top of him felt good. Their kiss went further as the desire to connect escalated.

Observing Tanner's need to feel him, Skye changed the position of his erection and pressed it tightly against Tanner where he knew he wanted it most. Feeling pressure, Tanner gasped as Skye's sturdy dick began tapping at his sucking asshole. Skye pushed harder into Tanner and the fit felt faultless.

Tanner looked into Skye's eyes and softly

spoke, "It's alright, Skye. I want to feel you."

Skye smiled and reached for the bottle of lube and a condom from the nightstand. He tore the wrapper open with his teeth and gave the condom to Tanner. "Go ahead and put it on me," he told him softly.

Before Skye lowered himself back down on top of Tanner, he stroked his covered dick with a lubricated hand.

While they kissed, Tanner rolled Skye onto his back and straddled him, pining for Skye to skewer his greedy hole.

Skye reached up, ran his hands across Tanner's muscular pectorals, and then moved them to his abs, feeling every raised ripple and every deep crease as the man sitting on him breathed.

Hungry to feel Skye inside him, Tanner lowered himself slowly until the part of Skye's body that was able to connect them together was sliding inside him.

Tanner's hands stroked Skye's chest while Skye speared him to complete the bond. Tanner's eyes closed until the torment of pure delight evolved into extreme desire. With moderate exertion, Tanner accepted the excessive pleasure of Skye's cock; the size of him reached a depth that had never been met before. They moved together, merging their bodies in a way that evoked undeniable pleasure, the amazing sensation of bursting growing in both men.

Skye could tell by the look on Tanner's face an orgasm was taking over his body. That was undeniable, but Skye wasn't ready to pull his cock out of Tanner's body yet. He wanted to stay deep inside Tanner, to keep fucking him, because he had more to give. To prevent them both from bursting, Skye ceased sliding his dick in and out of Tanner's tight channel. Cumming would end the pleasure they were giving each other. It was way too soon for that.

Skye gasped out his words, "Hold still, Tan... Don't move... Or I'm cumming in your ass." He inhaled sharply, squinted one eye and held his breath.

Tanner fell against Skye, kissing him, his breathing labored. "I almost came too... Fuck."

A few minutes passed before Skye was steady enough to say, "Okay... I'm good now. How 'bout you?"

Tanner sat back up, nodding, Skye's dick going deep when he did.

They rocked together. Tanner's abdomen flexed as he moved perpetually with Skye, though slower than before.

Transferring his grasp from Tanner's hips to his face, Skye told him how much he wanted him and that he could stay inside him forever.

Tanner agreed and his expression changed with every upward thrust of Skye's hips. An "Oh, fuck," escaped his corded throat every few thrusts.

With the warmth of Tanner's tight channel wrapped around him, Skye was forced to terminate his tempo again to prevent ejaculating too soon.

Leaning forward, Tanner huffed into Skye's ear. "You feel so fucking good in me, Skye." At the moment his climax started, he shuddered and groaned. "I think I'm falling in love with you, Skye," he gasped, feeling himself getting hot, and without touching himself, the churning inside him grew more powerful; about to boil over.

Skye held Tanner steady by the waist, his gasping cut short by Tanner's clutching heat. "I'm feeling the same, Tanner." He shivered, bit his lip, and squeezed his eyes closed.

Tanner stole his chest away from Skye's, moving up to fully straddle him, forcing Skye's cock to go deep and stay connected. He gasped when his orgasm surfaced.

Skye clasped his hands on Tanner's hips again, helping him maintain his dick-gripping momentum as he rode up and down on his rock hard cock.

Tanner tossed his head back, then jerked it forward. His body went tense and he groaned. His abdominal muscles crunched solid, helping pump his cum all over Skye's chest and face, some hitting the board above his head.

Then Skye's torso tightened, his shoulders snapped forward as his release found refuge inside Tanner's body where he wanted it. He groaned along with each spurt he shot from his cock.

Breathing heavily, they quaked, eyes fixed on each other, taking what the other was giving.

Tanner lowered his chest to Skye's and passionately kissed him.

While remaining tucked inside Tanner, Skye gave him a powerful hug as the last of his cum pumped from his cock.

As moments passed, they lay naked and connected, hanging on to one another while they kissed. Skye hugged Tanner hard again before lifting him from his chest. The white-hot cum that held them together turned clear and cool.

Tanner smiled down on Skye and then confided; "I've gotta have you to myself, Skye. No sharing you. Can you live with that?"

Looking up, Skye confessed; "I'd like that more than anything, Tanner. I'm glad you asked." He rolled his hips one more time to be sure he was empty, grunting while he did.

"Damn, you're a fucking cum stud." Staying seated a moment on Skye's cock until he was finished squeezing his spunk up his ass, Tanner regrettably pulled himself off of him, leaving Skye alone in the sun-filled room. Disappearing into the bathroom, Tanner blew Skye a kiss just before he closed the door.

Skye lay still, chest still dripping with the cum Tanner had left behind, treasuring his musky scent while glowing from the exhilaration of sharing his soul.

Chapter 24

Skye sat shirtless on the edge of the bed, wearing only a pair of pressed slacks that he would normally consider as attire for Easter Sunday. As much as he hated dressing up, he did it anyway when it was called for. He waited for Tanner to come out of the bathroom and when he did, the man looked masculine gay. A better description might be fucking gorgeous. How could one person be blessed with so many good genes? Tanner was one of those people.

Walking into the bedroom combing his hair with his fingers, Tanner asked, "Pants? Did you change your mind?"

"I gave it some thought and figured I can't let you go to an event this important alone." Skye stared at the muscles in Tanner's arms as he walked his way, watching the bulges jump as he lowered them to his sides.

Tanner dropped down next to Skye on the edge of the bed, kissed him, and took his hand.

"Thanks, Skye. It means a lot that you'll be with me tonight. I really want you there," he said to his lover.

Skye turned toward Tanner, bringing one knee up on the bed as he did. "I think I might be in love with you, Tanner. And so you know, I'm not saying that because you let me bury myself inside you, but because I enjoy being with you and I'd rather put your needs ahead of my own. I have an extreme desire to make sure you're happy. Always. I can't help the way I feel."

Looking intently at Skye, Tanner said, "After the way you made me feel in this bed, there's no denying we're meant for each other. What we shared was powerful, which makes me believe it had a lot to do with love. The other night when we were together, I fit perfectly inside you and today you connected with me just as flawlessly. Nobody has ever moved me the way you did, Skye. I don't ever want to live without that undeniable fact."

Skye kissed Tanner. It wasn't a lustful tongue-penetrating kiss, but one that was light and sensual. A chaste, emotional-filled kiss that meant; *I'm so totally in love with you.*

Slowly separating, Tanner said in a whispery tone, "As much as I'd rather stay and make love to you, the ball gown is waiting for me at the station."

"I'll be ready when we get home," Skye guaranteed him.

"You promise?"

"Count on it," Skye assured.

"It's a date." Tanner tweaked Skye's chin.

Skye nodded and inquired, "Would you like me to take you? Can you drive okay?"

Sneering as he stood, Tanner answered. "Listen, I've climbed ladders with broken toes. I've carried men over my shoulder with smoke in my lungs. What all that means is I'm a tough son-of-a-bitch. I think I'll be able to drive a car with a couple of bruises on my ankles."

Skye backed up. "Enough said; you win. Here, take your shirt and please put it on. If I look at you shirtless another second, I'll cream my pants."

"Taking care of me already, I like that." Tanner took the shirt from Skye. "Now it's your turn to put a shirt on before I ring your neck with another set of pearls like I did earlier." He leaned in for a hug.

"Whoa. What are you doing? Boner alert. Do not hug me without pants on. Do... Not... Hug me," Skye sputtered, backing away from the man he wanted to fuck again but didn't have time for.

"Okay, got it. Respect to you. But I've got you later," Tanner rambled, pointing a pistol finger at Skye.

"You got me. Any way you want me." Skye pistol-pointed back, feeling awkward when he did it.

Tanner put on the shirt Skye picked out for him. It was snug and he looked good in it, but that didn't matter, because it would be off soon anyway.

While Skye buttoned the over-starched shirt he had on, he said, "Tanner, is it okay with you if we go together?"

Tanner spun around, reaching for Skye's shirt to close the last button under his chin and jabbered,

"Certainly. Yes. I'd love that."

"Great. One glance in the mirror and we can go," Skye said.

On their way to the firehouse, a song that seemed suitable for the moment came on the satellite radio. It was a song Skye had always liked, so he sang *I'll Always Love You* along with the artist on the radio.

Tanner smiled when he heard Skye singing, thought it was cute, and then hummed the bottom while Skye sang the top.

Chapter 25

"This is where I let you go," Skye said while parking the car near the front entrance of the fire station. He wanted more than anything to kiss Tanner right there in the drive, a tongue-tangling kiss; but kept his lips sealed instead, because he was sure all eyes were on them.

Tanner sensed Skye's urge to lock lips with him, read the expression all over his face and knew he wouldn't have hesitated a second if Skye made his move right there in broad daylight. Tanner wasn't used to that part of Skye yet. The kissing only in dark alleys or behind closed doors. Tanner hadn't hidden who he was from anybody for such a long time that it felt strange to him, almost unnatural. He respected Skye's stoic public persona, because he remembered what it was like being in his shoes.

Under the influence of a fast-growing relationship, Tanner's head was about as cluttered as Skye's was, but with hardly any roadblocks. One thing Tanner thought about Skye every time he saw him was how damned beautiful he was. Fucking hot actually, in or out of clothes. Tanner studied Skye intently, he felt as if he'd burst if he took his eyes off him. He always wanted to touch Skye, hold his hand, kiss him, and be as close to him as humanly possible. More than that, he wanted to take Skye back home and make love to him like he'd promised he would before they left the house. He started getting a hard-on just thinking about it.

Tanner blinked away his fantasy so his dick would take a break. "Would you like to come in for a few minutes? You can watch me change," he suggested, lasciviously.

Skye greedily grinned. "Change into what? Is sci-fi for real? Are you planning to go all wolf-like on my ass or some crazy shit like that? Because if you are, make sure you have at me the same way that scorching hot Alfa character on television would. The good-looking one with the dark hair and body that can make a man go hard by simply glancing at him. I always seem to struggle with his name, can't pronounce it even with it spelled out in front of me. His name doesn't matter anyway; he's so fucking hot I'd fucking fuck him if he were within reach. I'd bet he'd like it if I did. Wait a sec, maybe I already have. Now that I think of it, you resemble him quite a bit. Holy shit, what's your real name?"

The corner of Tanner's mouth lifted. "I get it; you're obsessed with him, and with me. I was wondering when you were going to bring him up because I've heard that I look like him many times." Tanner leaned into Skye and growled, "So... am I to understand if I bear fangs, I can make my move?"

"As tempting as it sounds to have you wolf-hump my leg, I should let you go get ready by yourself. I'd only hold you up and they're probably in there waiting for you so they can get this thing started." One of Skye's brows lifted.

"I'll see you at the hall then."

"I wouldn't miss it."

Tanner held Skye's hand and squeezed it before saying, "I'll be watching for you, stud."

Skye responded with a tight-lipped smile.

Most of the lights in the hall were dimmed, leaving the brightest ones aimed at center stage where the firehouse captain stood and spoke, giving praise to every firefighter in the department. As time passed, one honorary award after another was handed to the deserving members. Piercing spotlight beams glared harshly in their faces the whole time. A hot fire they could tolerate, hot lights were a different story.

"As captain of SM-Three Fire Precinct, I have the pleasure of awarding our final cadet. I announce this one last because it's a distinct honor, not only for him, but for all of us at the station." The captain looked over his shoulder, scanning his entire team. "We welcomed this next cadet into our house, taking him in, facilitating his passion to fight fires and spare lives. I'd like to point out that it's never an easy thing being a firefighter; it's not.

There are challenges that come with the job that test a person's perseverance and endurance. This cadet accepted those challenges head-on, joining our team because he wanted to help others, save lives; pulling them from peril to keep them in this world where they belonged. Because there is so much passion within him, I had no choice but to honor him with the award as principal model of this firehouse. We're better for knowing him and from what I can see, we'll learn from this man's brave example. Please celebrate the graduation of our finest new firefighter." The captain stepped back, allowing Tanner to take the podium.

Without breaking stride on his way to the pedestal, Tanner, in his dress navy blues, white shirt and tie, looked stunning. He glanced around the room for Skye. When he spotted all the people in the hall except the man he really wanted to see, his heart sank a little, but he remained collected and spoke skillfully. Thanking many individuals, he added, "I joined this team to help people, rescue them from fires and dangerous situations, save them. The entire cadet experience has been a turning point in my life. It has cemented my understanding that I'm a part of something extraordinary. I've grown very close to everybody at the house, they will always be a part of my family, and I hope to remain a part of theirs. We're all tied together now, and if any of us move forward in separate directions, I damn well hope the bond we have will never be broken.

"One person I'd like to give great thanks to is my mentor and close friend, Lieutenant Emmitt Hansen. He's been instrumental in helping me reach the position I'm in right now, and was by my side through just about every step of my journey to this podium. Emmitt was there when I took the first step on that ladder, pushed me to the limits he knew I was capable of and was with me during every burn and scaring moment. For all you've done for and with me, Emmitt, I thank you. I love you, brother."

Tanner turned and grinned at the guys behind him, waiting for the roaring to make its way to the rafters and back down again. Turning back to the crowd, he finished by saying, "People are always asking me how is it that firefighters can run into burning buildings when everyone else is running out? My answer is always the same: courage. So I tell you this; next time that bell rings, we'll be back on the truck, because this team is the bravest and most courageous of them all and damn if I'm not proud to be a part of it."

Tanner glanced around the room and found Skye along the back wall looking directly at him. Their gazes connected. Tanner stared at him intently and suddenly it was personal. The thought that ran through his head just about knocked his legs out from under him. He could have stopped there. Maybe should have, but Skye's auburn eyes, practically glowing under the lights, said everything was going to be okay. There was something in Skye's expression, perhaps his smile that just kept getting brighter, telling Tanner to go with whatever he was planning to say next. The first word that came to Tanner's mind was irresistible, but he hesitated before continuing. "There is one special person I'd like to share this honor with. He's not sitting here among all these guys behind me, but somebody out there who I helped survive a recent fire." Tanner looked at Skye again, watching him bite his lip and then gracefully nod.

Tanner unexpectedly unclipped the microphone from the podium, taking it with him as he left the stage to make his way through the crowd of family members, friends, and acquaintances. "It's probably an uncommon dedication, I don't know, but I'd like to share this moment with my newest friend and closest companion." Tanner stopped when he reached Skye, placing a hand on his shoulder. "The one I want to share this with is standing right here, the man who became part of my life the day I helped him from the embers that mysteriously brought us together. Since that day, which I truly believe was meant to be, this man, Skye, *is* the piece in my life that's been missing and it would mean the world to me if you would share this moment with me."

Skye had a big grin on his face when everybody in the hall hooted some weird woofing noises after Tanner finished his acceptance speech and dedication. Skye was sure most of the noise was for Tanner, he himself was there as the guest of honor and a survivor of a death drop from two stories up. Skye might very well been amazed at how much these guys cared about each other, for Tanner. Skye recognized their bond as tighter than one he'd ever seen. They seemed like the type of guys who wouldn't care if he let loose or stood a little closer to the man he was falling in love with. He'd love to take that chance, be courageous, but his mind was too busy making sure he didn't accidentally grab hold of Tanner's hand or move in for that kiss he really wanted. He battled his inner desires to remain discreet.

While the noise level in the room was settling, Tanner leaned into Skye's ear and whispered so only he could hear, "This might be awfully soon to say, but I love you desperately, Skye."

When Tanner pulled away and smiled, Skye made a spontaneous decision to say a few words in spite of his worry about what everybody might think. He reached for the microphone still in Tanner's hand, making sure their fingers touched, then nodded again like he was giving himself approval to say what was on his mind. He tapped the mic's crown like everybody seems to do before speaking into it and then said, "Thank you, Tanner, for that marvelous introduction."

Surprised by the sudden turn of events, everybody looked at Skye, who suddenly felt invincible. Turning to Tanner, Skye continued, "It wasn't expected, but I couldn't be happier that you included me in your dedication, and if it's alright, I'd like to sneak up on stage for a moment if I may."

Everyone on the floor near Skye stepped aside, making a pathway that led to the podium. Some coaxed him with a hand against his back, pushing him along so they could hear what he had to say.

"Wow. Here I am, unexpectedly on stage. Woo, I never saw that coming." Skye glanced at his feet, looking for confidence. "Like Tanner said earlier, this is probably a dedication out of the ordinary and just might be a first. I'd like to start by thanking Tanner for dragging me out of that fire the other day. I'm pleased to be alive, and I can't imagine if he hadn't been the one who saved me. He's truly a hero to me and somebody I find to be rightfully extraordinary." Skye looked at Tanner. Tanner gave the go-ahead nod, the one Skye needed so he knew whatever happened next, it would be all right. "I'm proud of Tanner for a lot of reasons. Not only because of the many people he has already saved and will save in the future, but how much he really cares for them when he does it. If Tanner knows it or not, he saved me from more than just a fiery pit of doom, he showed me that I can be strong during tough situations, find my way through those hard times, and come out of them feeling good about myself.

"Because Tanner did that for me and gave me the one thing in my life I've been missing, too, I want to thank him by accepting his generous dedication as well as let him know that he's more than just my personal hero. He knows exactly what I'm talking about and you'll soon find out what I mean.

"In conclusion, I'd like to give well-deserved congratulations to MY boyfriend, who is standing right... back... there." Skye pointed at Tanner, set the microphone on the pedestal with a clumsy thump, and made his long overdue journey to the back of the room where he kissed Tanner on the mouth while everyone in the room watched.

With their lips locked, Tanner muttered; "Why'd you do it?"

"Because I love you." Skye spoke into Tanner's smiling mouth.

Tanner kissed him back and mumbled; "Just remember who said it first."

Epilogue

Looking viciously hot in a suit and tie, Emmitt met Skye and Tanner in the doorway of the hall with a glass of wine in each hand. "Looks like you two might need these. Drink and enjoy, it'll take the edge off," he said, handing the glasses over.

Skye nearly broke the glass when he seized it from Emmitt. "Oh, Gawd, sorry." He held it with both hands, afraid that if he didn't, somebody might take it from him.

Tanner took his glass smoothly because he felt no obligation to hide his desire for Skye from anybody in the room. He had an emotional involvement with Skye, one that would eventually show itself in the light of day and not just among friends.

"So, guys... When's the wedding? I'm dying to be your man of honor," Emmitt asked, with a laugh.

GJS

ABOUT THE AUTHOR

Gregory Jonathan Scott was born and raised in Grand Rapids, Michigan. Shortly out of high school was when he began his longtime relationship with his partner and companion Scott. Having artistic hands, together they pursued building a small business in ceramic art and pottery that quickly grew into the number one distribution center for hobbyists, storefronts and scholastic industries. During that time, Gregory was approached by art magazines to write short articles and educational columns pertaining to the ceramic artistry. After charming readers by his writing style, it ignited his desire to express himself further. From there, it began. Finding a love for writing, alongside his artistic hand, gave him inspiration to design and write M/M romance Novels that captivate and take the reader on unexpected adventures.

Gregory and Scott are still together and are currently enjoying home life in South Florida with their lovable Shetland sheepdog and a sweet stray cat.

OTHER WORKS BY
Gregory Jonathan Scott

CRASHING INTO LOVE
THE PLANTATION AFFAIR
HEARTBREAK BEAT

TAKE TO THE SKY SERIES
TAKE TO THE SKY – 1ST BOOK
(COMING SOON)
INTO THE HEADWINDS – 2ND BOOK

Encouraged By Sparks